Quirky Tales To Ma

A collection of short
Henthorn

For Mark and Alicia.

A Preamble for 'Quirky Tales'

Thank you for considering to read my short story collection. I hope you enjoy them as much as I have enjoyed writing them during the past eighteen months. Stories are a way of processing imagination, regurgitating it into a light and quirky way of looking at life's challenges, tales and 'what-ifs'. These stories are mostly general fiction, with overtones of tragicomedy. Aliens on the beach in Brighton, three teenage girls find some sweets in a lift, Kurt Cobain's ghost, Cézanne's wife, the survival struggle of a lone earthworm; to name but a few. Two of these stories were entered into competitions, both making the long list. Two of which are samples from my forthcoming novels '1962' and 'Curmudgeon Avenue'.

Due to longstanding health problems, I found myself in a position where I was forced to make life changing decisions. It's been a battle, I need a break, a chance to escape and an opportunity to justify my existence. I found myself at a local library, completing a two-year Creative Writing class. I joined a writing group, and now I am accidentally embarking on an English Literature and Creative Writing (BA honours) with the Open University. I had to make a choice, it was either write or become a rock star. Unfortunately, everyone knows that becoming a rock star is a young man's game (of which I am neither), so I have decided to go for it with this collection before my spirit is broken in the literary leg of my studies.

During my time listening to my writing friend's short stories and poetry, I often feel it a shame that these efforts will not reach their literary destiny. I would like to take this opportunity to thank the Whitefield Writing Circle, the Irwell Writers and Bury Library services and Adult Learning Service. Also big thanks to Lyndsey Prince for the illustrations. Who am I to disappoint my quirky tales by locking them away in a drawer, never to be read?

Happy reading, enjoy! ... Samantha

1) American Elevator
2) Hate
3) Midget Gems
4) Summer is the Best Time for Ambition
5) The Washing Machine Diaries (an Excerpt)
6) To Kill Two Birds
7) Pogonophobia
8) V is for Very
9) Pretty Scary
10) One Small Step
11) The Witch Hunt
12) The Storm in a Teacup
13) The Reminder
14) Swimmingly
15) Night Time Wonderings
16) Qu'est-ce que c'est
17) Tangling
18) The Mystery of Sight
19) Madame Cézanne
20) Safari Type Trip
21) Italian Elvis
22) Cringe-Worthy People
23) The Causeway
24) A Fresh Start
25) Finding the Right Name
26) Spoofapedia

American Elevator

'It has been fifteen years, one month and ten days since we increased our security procedure' His echoing repetition increased every twenty-four hours. Seemingly someone stupid had not observed the rules, disregarded seriousness, resulting in a queue.
'If you can't comply with these conditions, we cannot allow you access to our facility'
The length of the queue, her escape moment opportune.
'You know I don't like heights!' She hissed, not a fan of skyscrapers, or steep inclines it's true, she missed the point of the tourist attraction's defences.
'You can't leave me! It would look odd for a husband without his wife, with views to see, up high!'
She pleaded to stay downstairs, in amongst the tourists. The vast and tempting gift shop with far too much to choose. He disagreed quite righteously... insisting she accompanies him, her vertigo denied.

As they shuffled through the metal detector arch, the officious security man's mantra regarding the length of time 'Fifteen years' and so on, dragged them further along the queue. Increased security, confidence undermined. Lines, only humans form them, and only tourists would queue for an elevator, a fancy lift to the sky. The perfect place for people watching peering eyes glancing, accusing:

'Who?'

Holidaymakers herded like cattle. Most with a companion, apart from one odd occasional tourist who is standing right behind her. He is from Alaska and reports:

'I don't get out often' to anyone within earshot. Odd occasional tourist makes eye contact, presumes she is alone.

'Tell me, are you visiting Seattle for business or pleasure?'

'Excuse me?'

'I said, are you here for business or pleasure?'

His question open ended, she swiftly closed with 'NO!' The woman had never been so pleased to see her husband return from the restroom. The odd occasional tourist had not expected romance quashed, dreams dashed. You see; elevators are great places to meet people, he had read that somewhere (someplace) It had been fifteen years since the odd occasional tourist had met *any*one.

An attitude of teenage backpackers travelling no further than outside the U.S. over excited, peaking too soon, speaking too loudly, and reporting on pointless smartphone applications.

'Look, this one works out your 'stripper name' *BLAH BLAH, BLAH, BLAH BLAH.* I didn't know that Bali is not part of India!' Their nonsense lost towards the end of the line.

The security mantra softens in the distance, dollars exchanged for tickets - reluctantly accepted. Feeling dizzy already at the sight of those lift doors, their dull shine, their promise of space fearfully anticipated, eagerly embraced, by her husband alone.

'Don't look up, and do not look down!'

The elevator holds ten tourists, all of reasonable weight. The collective ten play happy families for less than a moment. The 500ft takes forty-one seconds, except on days that are windy on which it takes longer, the brochure threatens. Her suspicion raised, the needle has stood for over fifty years - but does that make it safe? She buries her head in his chest, silently counts to forty-one, like an elongated game of hide and seek. The powerful rush, the strange sensation, the elevator catapults the tourists into the air with inexplicable physics. Those forty-one seconds seemed twice as long. So worried, that she did not even notice the beautiful attendant, smartly dressed, skin like an Easter egg. But a middle-aged woman certainly did, along with her giggling counterpart.

'Well ain't you somethin' honey!' The woman did not blush from underneath her sun visor. 'The Space Needle was built in 1962, for the 'World Fair" The beautiful attended repeated, with little time for his speech.

'Do you enjoy your job?' The woman asked, managing plenty of time to flirt.

'It has its ups and downs' He smirks with perfect teeth, and then it's time to get out.

She is still buried in her husband, the flirting woman pushes past. She walks backwards out of the elevator, legs like jelly, stomach in her mouth. She is not the only one to be adversely affected, a sobbing, shaking middle-aged man is dragged out by his wife.

'I'll just wait here, over by the door, where I feel safe, maybe sit on the floor,' She says. He looks dismayed, but leaves her there, not wishing to waste those dollars. He marks his visit on the map. He takes in the view, the expanse of water, miles, and miles can be seen under miles and miles of cloud, are those mountains in the distance? After a couple of solitary self-portraits on the observation deck (saluted by the odd occasional tourist), It is time to rescue his wife, she is standing by the elevator, eyes firmly shut, head cradled in her hands.

'My brain is swimming, I feel so dizzy, It's all your fault of course!'

They go back to the start, the same whooshing sound accompanies them to the ground.

Reuniting with gravity, the best bit of the day for her. He is oblivious to the sensation, insisting she buys a T-shirt or a keychain at least to prove he '*got her on that elevator!*'

It feels like fifteen years since they visited Seattle.

They say it will get better, with therapy and graded exposure. She will not engage, however, with confined spaces that have no way of escape. Her acute case of acrophobia, claustrophobia, stranger danger, husband blamed catastrophe.
Fifteen years, and still no official name for 'fear of elevators'.

Hate

I have never liked being patronised, I mean, who does? You must know what I'm talking about... Those people who adopt fake posh accents, whilst simultaneously undermining your ability to understand. As though you are an imbecile, unable to cope without their unsolicited advice. Self-doubt producing talk promotes the patronising person's strength and superiority. I don't know how they do it. I don't know how they sleep at night. I never say anything at the time. I'm too nice. I've spent years and years talking to myself, ruminating over imaginary conversations about what I *should have* said to them; whoever 'they' are.

I went to my GP, I've been having trouble sleeping, and do you know what he said? 'Have I tried mindfulness?'

They (whoever 'they' are) have done some research and found that this mind altering technique is more effective, more beneficial than any drug or talking therapy available. Everyone is doing it. Whoever 'everyone' is. I've read about it on social media, people reporting how good mindfulness is, then the next day reporting how stressed out they are.

'Why don't I go to the Buddhist Centre in Manchester and learn how to do it?' The GP had said.

End of appointment.

He was obviously not listening in medical school on the day they learned about multiple sclerosis. Because, for me, going to the city is like running a marathon. Out of the question. Why should I have to learn mindfulness? I've got an alternative:

1) Stop being a people pleaser.

2) Cut stress off at the source, waste no further time with negative people.

3) Spend all week looking after myself.

4) Enjoy life at the weekend.

Gradually, things start to get better. I look after myself on weekdays wearing a variety of pyjamas, or, on days when I have physiotherapy, fitness gear. I make an appointment with myself to have a rest day (which 'they' used to try and get me to cancel) I go out at the weekend - provided I feel up to it. It's a full-time job managing myself, so exhausting.

The only problem is, 'They' don't know about the plan. 'They' won't leave me alone. 'They' want to come round, drink my tea, tell me all about their mother-in-law, and how the NHS would crumble, should 'They' have to take early retirement on health grounds (like-what-I-did) 'They' then say something judgemental like:

'I'll leave you now so that you can carry on watching TV- oh it's alright for some!'
JOG ON.

'They' eventually leave me alone. But there's always one. Always one, making my ears burn, popping into my head intuitively making me think; are 'They' gossiping about me? Those who gossip to you will gossip about you, that's what 'They' say. Oh! *They'* are back again.
DO ONE.

Later that same day, my husband returned home and said that some woman had telephoned him on his mobile.

'She sounded posh, gets on the phone to me, whilst I was in the middle of something. Starts asking how you are. Says she's concerned about you!'
'WHAT?'

'Yeah, I didn't know who she was talking about at first because she used your Sunday name, and to be honest, I don't have time for crap like that when I'm trying to work'
'Work? Anything good on YouTube today husband?...What did you say to her?'
'I didn't get the chance to say owt, it was that Laura one, she said she needs to pop round and see you'
'NO! NO! She is not ... No, she doesn't *need* to pop round! OH I feel so anxious'
'Well, what was I supposed to say? Just ring her and tell her you don't want her to come round'
'NO! No way, if I say that to her, she'll accuse me of being depressed! Just because I don't want to see her, doesn't mean there's something up with me!'
I tried to hurry downstairs, I cello taped my '*PLEASE DO NOT DISTURB*' sign to the inside of the front door window.
'Please, do not speak to her again' I was out of breath by the time I got back upstairs, it was like running a marathon.
....

The following day, I had an appointment at the hospital. It was strange because I had never had an appointment with this doctor before. I usually see a neurologist. Weirdly, this doctor had the same surname as a psychiatrist from the same mental health unit I used to work at.

The consultant thumbed through my medical notes, I could read his face like a text message, he had just noticed that my occupation was 'Registered Mental Health nurse' I saw the penny drop and imagined a 'shocked face' emoji.

He cleared his throat.

I don't want to bore you, I was asked lots of questions, they go right into your childhood on those assessments. I was feeling uncomfortable. He wasn't asking me the right questions. Neurologists are usually concerned with how many times you've fallen, how fast you can walk, that sort of thing. Then my penny dropped, this was not a neurology appointment. I wanted to change the subject, clear things up, try and explain I was in the wrong department. I knew how to get out of it, but what I really needed this doctor to ask me was:

'Did I know why I was here?' Then I could have escaped.

I didn't even get the chance to tell him that my husband was parking the car. Just as he was getting on to the bit where he asks me if I've ever been sexually abused, I stop him in his tracks.

'Can I just ask you what I'm doing here?'

He looked at me over the top of his spectacles as though I've gone completely bonkers.

'I mean, I usually see a neurologist about my MS, who referred me to you?'

There was lots more thumbing through paper notes, clicking on keyboards and clearing of throats.

'Well, actually, I have a letter here from a Laura Whale, saying she is an ex-colleague of yours, she is an RMN, however, so we had to take her concerns seriously'

'WHAT?'

'It's all above board, your GP was fine with the referral, he actually added a note to say you have reported insomnia to him recently' He said, clearing his throat again 'You've attended at your own free will, however. Are you happy to continue?'

'What? No! Laura? Laura Whale? No! Please let me explain... I have this plan, right'

I told him the whole thing about my 'four-point plan' but that it was difficult because 'They' didn't know about it. How I had to pretend I wasn't at home sometimes and bought a *'DO NOT DISTURB'* sign especially for the front door. I was trying to explain, and he was giving me nothing back. Except that every time I said 'they' he kept jotting something down in my notes. And occasionally he would say:

'Right' and then clear his throat.

I wasn't making much sense, and to make matters worse, I had started crying. The worst kind of crying. I was sobbing, and gasping for breath, with tears and snot all over my face. He passes me a wafer thin handkerchief from an NHS tissue box. I took more than one, and bury my face in the two-ply confetti making material (must remember not to leave this in my tracksuit pocket)

I gather my strength together, but this makes me feel all angry and 'stressy' like the spiky ward sister from the day hospital downstairs where I used to work.

Inhale. Exhale. He takes this as a sign that I am ready to go on.

 This was the most awkward situation I had ever been in. He knows who I am, and I know who he is...

'I need to ask you have you ever had any thoughts of killing yourself?'

'NO!' My voice doesn't get as loud as I want it to anymore.

'What about other people? Have you ever had thoughts of harming them?'

Well, I told him all about it, didn't I? How 'They' were treating me like I'm stupid, telephoning my husband saying 'They' are concerned about me. That sort of thing, well he kept asking me questions, approaching my risk of harm to others from all different angles, until I finally admitted:

'Yes. Yes I have had thoughts of harming others, well one person really, but only in self-defence'

The consultant was scribbling away. I had started saying 'They' again.

'I mean, if she does come round to my house, I would grab one of my walking sticks, hit her over the head and then ... I don't know, grab her by the hair and knock her head against the wall'

'Right'

'Well, you asked... it's only a thought... there's nothing wrong with thoughts is there? I mean, if I hit someone with my walking stick, I would probably fall over, and anyway, there are too many bins in the way to hit her head against the wall'

'Bins?'

'Four bins we've got at our house'

'Right'

'It's all the recycling'

He took his spectacles off and rubbed his eyes with his forefinger and thumb. Maybe he was getting a headache, but then he cleared his throat and had another question for me.

'Ok, would you be willing to have a rest in the psychiatric unit?'

'What? No! I'm going home!'

'Wait here please, I need to go to the other office and make a phone call' The consultant opened the door.

'Is my husband out there? He is used to the neurology department' I said, but it was as though I hadn't spoken.

I knew what he was doing. He was speaking to the hospital gatekeepers to arrange a bed, and another approved mental health professional to say that I needed the admission that I'd refused. Hopefully, it would be a social worker and I could explain to them that this was all a misunderstanding. They will probably know Laura themselves because she is a dinosaur and they will probably have wanted to kill her at some point too...

The consultant was back in the room, looking all flustered.

'I'm afraid I haven't been able to get hold of any of my approved colleagues it's all the bank holidays... but I do think that you need emergency admission to the psychiatric unit, so I've arranged a bed for you. I will ask you one more time: will you be admitted on a voluntary basis?'

'No, I will not!' I folded my arms, sucked in my cheeks and stuck my nose in the air.

'I'm going to admit you under what we call section four of the mental health act, this is an emergency section which lasts for seventy-two hours.'

'I know what section four is!... It's bad practice!' I pout.

Maybe he doesn't recognise me after all? I notice him scribble the word 'grandiose' in my notes.

There ensued police assistance, shouting, folding of arms, scribbling in notes, threats to report the consultant to the General Medical Council. I was even manhandled at one point, and my husband was nowhere to be seen... I didn't see him until I was sitting in a single room with a glass observation panel in the door. Embarrassingly on the same ward that I used to work on. He had been given a talk about how this was 'for the best' and I would be assessed in more detail as an inpatient. 'Please get me out of here' was the first thing I said to him.

'They've asked me to go fetch your toothbrush and a change of clothes. Oh and not to bring anything valuable because it'll get nicked, it's like you're in prison! You could've texted me to tell me which department you were in, I was waiting for you at neurology like a lemon!'

'OH,' I sighed 'Mobile phones don't work inside the hospital' Which made me have a flashback to when I was working with Laura. One day she left me inside the main hospital with a patient for hours and hours, and then she harsh-tongued me for switching my mobile off, except I hadn't switched it off, mobile phones don't work inside the hospital. This was all her fault, I'm definitely going to kill her.

I did not sleep well that night. My husband was ushered out of the ward because visiting times were over. I refused to go to the canteen to get something to eat. The toilets were disgusting. The nursing station was right outside my bedroom window. Shining in my direction like the world's nosiest night light. I could see the night nurse sitting there, I was on 'suicide watch' and she was reading a 'celebrity' magazine. I must have fallen asleep at some point though because the sound of assertive door knocking woke me. Where was I? Before I had the chance to react, keys were jangled and the door was opened.

'Visitor for you, love!' the suicide watcher barked.

'Hello Suzanne, I've been concerned about you...' Laura Whale was standing in the doorway.

She wasn't standing for long, though, I can tell you.

Midget Gems

I took a deep breath and knocked on the door. That's what Shona told me to do, 'Don't let your Nan or your Mam smell your breath, they'll be able to tell we've been drinking' That's what she'd said before she ran off down Coconut Grove. We'd ran and ran, then waited around for someone to let me in with their fob key. Running for our lives, but I don't know why. It's tomorrow now and I'm not going to bed, I'm in no rush, but OMG! How fast could we run last night! Well funny... I don't think I'm ever going to sleep again... I'd better breathe now... I've been waitin' ages now... I'd better breathe... It's a million years since Shona and Kelly and me ran down ... ran down?... OMG, where did we lose Kelly? OH, Shiiiii....ugar!

'What time do you call this? Missy?'

I swear my Nan puts on an Irish accent when I'm in trouble.

'Lost your key again, is it? Get in! I'm warning you, don't let your mother see!'

Her words shoved me in, and then she was behind me. Windows, colours, June sunlight, my beautiful Nan's purple veins, I never noticed how blue her eyes are before, wow! I never noticed you can see right through her dyed hair, grey spider's webs shining through the maroon. She always rolls her house coat sleeves up when she answers the door, to show off tattoos on her forearms. Makes her look hard.

'WELL?' Nan sort of shout-y whispered, then her face changed like the devil in her had noticed the devil in me.

'Jesus child, open your eyes, stop squinting!' I put my face in hers and popped my eyes open wide like Shona told me not to. Don't think it's alco-pop death breath we need worry about... it's Kelly... we've lost her.

'Look what you've done now! See! You've woke your mother up'

Mam pushed Nan out of the way.

'We've been up all night worried sick about you' Mam lied, wiping the sleep out of her eyes with her onesie sleeve. 'Where's that letter to the council, Mam?' She turned on Nan, Mam has it too, the colours 'We've got to get out of this shit-hole, get us a place up Seddon, or back on Magpie court'

'I'm goin finding Kelly'

But the door was blocked by my Mam. The door; our door with a hole booted in by Ste, I was seven then, and he don't come round no more. Nan lost her flat, they reckon it's the government and bedroom tax, she's been on our settee ever since.

....

You know when it goes slow motion on the telly? When they do the replays on the footy? Well, that's what it looked like then. They kept looking at me, then looking at each other, then back to me again, peering in my face and right into my eyes. Then they turned to each other mouthing 'definitely' nodding in agreement, with matching dyed hair (different each week because it depends what colour Mam's mate can nick from Superdrug) Dressed like twins, with their fake gel nails of shiny magenta, that are three for the price of two from Stella across the way (don't tell the benefits)... Not gonna look like them when I'm older... do one Stella! You can keep your 'three for twos'... Mascara in the mirror, streaked down my face right to my chin. And they were laughing... laughing at me... are you laughing at me?

Nan knew what to do. Soon I was lying on top of the sheets on my bed being force fed water.

'What about Kelly?' I cried, but Nan was gone, I thought about jumping out the window to find her... I thought about sleep. I thought about a lot of things, how fast does your mind run on these? I had some great ideas, I should've written down. We were only supposed to be going round Shona's to chill. Her mam and dad pull the settee out on the front the second the weather gets hot. *I feel hot now.* Her mam is really into getting a tan. Her dad makes the same joke every day 'Costa del Salford' laughing to himself, with his disposable barbeque.

The sun is coming out again, I think about the sun, about reaching for the light, and flashbacks from last night; the lift where we live next to the precinct. Only place round 'ere you don't need a reference Nan says. Meet some right crack-eds in that boneshaker. This guy in a stripy t-shirt winked at me, made me feel funny. Then his mobile rang:

'Yeah I saved some personal'

When he pulled his hand out of his pocket, summat fell out, and when he got out on the third floor, I picked up a tiny packet that looked like them sweets, midget gems but with proper bogus stamps on them. I shoved them in my pocket and when me and Kelly got to Shona's, we all knew what they were, except Kelly, but she soon knew. It's in fashion again, droppin' pills like in the nineties. It was well funny, how fast can you run on E's? Now I look at my smashed phone screen and wake up to permanent shame, a thousand selfies on Instagram, bottom jaws grinding, sweating our tits off, reaching for the lights. I see our block with its fifth floor burnt out windows on the news. Our block. Not the first time our block has made headlines, they said we were:

'Thought to be the youngest people ever to take Ecstasy. One girl has been admitted to hospital and is thought to be in a critical state'...

I've found Kelly! I know where she is now, I'm coming down now, it's wearing off now. I found Kelly and so did the ambulance man... on his night shift... in his ambulance, shaking his head, he took a deep breath and opened the door.

Summer is the Best Time For Ambition. After much verbal manipulation during the early months of 1962, Mr Potts the greengrocer finally succumbed to Rose Bradshaw's persuasion. Albeit a quiet person, when it came to her son Ernest, Rose would perpetually nest and nurture using a skill that could rival any member of the animal kingdom. In spring, the seeds she had sown began to take root and her son, Ernest was soon to be employed by Mr. Potts as the bicycle delivery boy. The majority of the deliveries were conveyed in his van, but the cottages on Lever Brew had proven to be virtually inaccessible on four wheels. The folk that lived there would have to do their shopping on their own two feet! As much as Mr. Potts wanted to say no to Rose (he had his reasons) he eventually said yes to employing her son in 'pocket money job'. Maybe this year things would be different.

Now, British summertime begins officially when the clocks change at the end of March. A relic from days of war and farming domination. The weather, however, does not automatically follow. Ernest Bradshaw set out on a wintry March day, on the ancient low gravity Hercules carrier bike he began to nurture his own packet of dreams. Dreams that would burst into blooming bounty during June and July. The loaned cycle was designed and fit for purpose, the front wheel smaller to accommodate a basket. It was heavy, to begin with. Add to that Ernest's fourteen-year-old body, basket and side pannier bags filled with pounds upon pounds of potatoes, and the Hercules bicycle became a herculean challenge. Ernest, with his mother's determination behind him, although wobbly at first soon found he could manage. His little white legs, white knuckles, jaw set, chin pointing forward pushed down the pedals. Round and round they went, up and down, goods delivered, wages pocketed. Ernest had never had money before and did not know what to do with nearly a whole pound every week. April came and went, apple blossoms blew in his face and stuck to his glasses. Youthful athleticism on his side, Ernest's stamina grew, improved. He could not say he had ever really noticed summer before. The dewy scent of sunrise, the singing birds, the layers shed. When he started his round the sky was still dawn coloured, when he finished, it was light. His mother, Rose awaited and anticipated summer every year.

'There's nowt better than a British summertime' She would say, but it was always over far too soon. However, for a fourteen-year-old Ernest, long summer days became long summer months. Time enough to nurture his budding ambition. By May, Ernest's confidence began to vegetate. He had moved on from 'managing' the deliveries, to dispatching them with ease. His customers appeared impressed. Mr Ainsworth from one of the cottages said to him

'EEEE Ernest! Ever thought of putting in for th'Olympic team on that bike?'

And that was all Ernest needed. His backbone fertilised, soon flourished into dreams of winning imaginary cycle races. 'I'm getting good at this,' he said to himself. One of his school masters had said to the class that everybody, every single one of them had a talent, they just had to find it in themselves. The green grass, the green leaves, everything that summer touched blossomed. And as the solstice sun of June freckled up his legs, face, and arms, nothing could go wrong. On his first round in July, Mr Potts told Ernest he was the

'Fastest delivery boy on two wheels'

Mr Brown, the butcher swilling out his bucket in the back entry overheard this and soon asked Ernest to deliver for him. Bacon and braising steak in brown paper. Like the tomato plant in Mr. Tower's greenhouse, Ernest's round branched off in several directions. One by one, the proprietors of the high street employed him. His growing round easily managed in the summer school holidays.

Ernest was proud of his abilities, a secret garden in his own mind. But one heady Sunday at Auntie Marigold and Uncle Norman's, Ernest was asked what he planned to do when he left school. Drunk on homemade honey and elderflower cordial, Ernest blurted out:

'I'm going to join the Great Britain Olympic cycling team!'

The grownups laughter withered him, even deaf Uncle Billy laughed. Later on, Auntie Marigold was reading something out from yesterday's newspaper, the Manchester Guardian about the 'bay of pigs' it was all still going on. His mother could be overheard saying that she had warned Ernest not to 'sing his own praises' and that he 'had no right coming out with such fanciful ideas'. Uncle Norman approached Ernest who was pulling the petals off a sunflower, hanging limp, defeated by the breeze.

'Ernest, if you're serious about cycling I can perhaps introduce you to a chap I sometimes see drinking in the pub. You'll know him, Harry Hill'

'Who?' Ernest asked. His mother always said that Uncle Norman is a 'know it all' but Ernest could not see the harm in knowing things.

'Yes, Harry Hill, He's a local hero! He won bronze, you know, cycling in the 1936 Olympics!'

'Well, I wasn't alive then Uncle' Perhaps Uncle Norman didn't know everything.

'I know lad, but that doesn't mean it didn't happen. I reckon if you get your training in for the rest of the summer, you'll be ready for one of those cycle races you see on Sundays in September. Bloody nuisance they are, have to take the car round a different way if the wife wants to visit your mother'

Well, Ernest could not wait to get on his two wheeled friend. Cycling nurtured all summer and harvested by winning a race in September. Summer truly is the best time for ambition.

The Washing Machine Diaries (an excerpt)

Returning on a rainy Monday mid-morning in August. I hear their engine deaden, then relieved. A key in the door and the silence is no more. Hollow house plants stand to attention, it is now our turn to perform. Sleeping bags are dragged, like slugs, then he slides them across the laminate floor. She is glad to be home and embraces her cherished white goods like a fool.*'Hello fridge, hello dishwasher! Hello toilet, Oh, I mustn't forget you! Helloooo washing machine, am I glad to see you'*

Without the chance to limber up, washing away the weekend commences. The annual summer reminder of youth. What goes up, must come down and like a pair of cold turkeys released into the wild, it's written all over their faces, that they've 'had it large'. They are British, and this is what they do. I'm stationed in the deepest, darkest corner of the dungeon that is the garage conversion. The first of many dark cycles commences. She shoves the sorry sleeping bag into the drum, shoves it! Protruding and deflating like the last balloon of a children's party. Detergent in the drawer, and carelessly sprinkled on the floor. She is usually particular and separates laundry into mountains of lights, darks, and delicates but not today, they need to be washed away. Invariably wary not to overload, especially wet towels. Strained motor prevented, phew! On days past, should a stray tissue remain up his sleeve, or in his jeans, there would be hell to pay. Do not tell anyone, but last week she turned the air blue *'You imbecile!'* she had screamed like a teenager, face screwed up as though she had tasted something sour. But she is not paying attention today, and my hopes are pinned on zero inanimate objects intruding the laundry's pockets. I dread a plume of tissue confetti in the air, and imitation dandruff on her clothes, it would be all his fault of course. The following pile of laundry is neither sorted or unravelled. Evidential burger sauce paints his jeans, a T-shirt she is too old for, a sagging advertisement for a band no longer heard. Underwear and socks fermented, should be discarded, but reluctantly accepted. Should I turn one pyjama leg inside out just for fun? I'd better not... Textile care labels rebelliously overlooked, resulting in knickers now the colour of 'chewing gum grey'. They steal mud from anywhere to bring the outdoors in. The faint reminder of porta-loos laundered and forgotten. Round and round, rinse, drain, spin, dry, fold, put away again.

To Kill Two Birds

Harold and Edith live in a 1970s bungalow in suburbia.
Climbing Ivy, they had planted years ago wound around their garden fence like regretful, parasitic life suckers. They had quarrelled about it, but Edith had sacked the gardener.
Their accumulative age is around one hundred and forty-five. Harold is seventy-three, and ten days old. Their daily routine is important to them and every morning they would read the headlines in '*The Daily Judgement'* newspaper.
'BREXIT BRITAIN', 'BENEFITS BRITAIN', 'BROKEN BRITAIN' And best of all: **'WHO'S TAXES ARE PAYING FOR IT?'**
On the day this all started, the sky was full of August apologies for a summer undelivered. Harold's goggle eyes darted about under his spectacles, he smacked his lips together and his neck wobbled like a turkey.
'I see that for sale sign next door says 'SOLD' I'll be glad to see the back of Mr and Mrs Roscoe'

'Oh! I hope the new people don't have children!' Edith's fingers clenched around the neckline of her nightdress. Children were feared the most by Edith.

'What the bloody hell is that noise? They've moved a bit sharpish haven't they?' Harold stood up from the breakfast table to address the rumble of a removal van. He folded the newspaper, pinching it into a neat, crisp line. Edith mulled over the next headline:

'INCREASE IN FATAL HOUSEHOLD ACCIDENTS'

'They want to do something about that!' Edith cried out, as if 'they' could ever do anything. Harold was now peeping through the smooth of the frosted glass in their bungalow's porch.

'Hello, neighbour!' A voice boomed 'I'll come over later and introduce myself proper! Platt's the name!'

'Oh crikey Edith, he's seen me! The bugger's seen me! Said his name is Pratt!' Harold skated back down the hall, his slippers providing extra purchase 'Hide!'

They hid under their kitchen table for longer than was reasonably necessary. Regrets of a dismissed gardening service consumed them as they counted the fallen leaves collecting on the patio... to their horror, the new neighbour's face appeared over the top of their fence.

'This fence wants replacing! I noticed it when we had the survey done!'

Silence from indoors.

'Oi! There's a hole in this fence! I think your tree's done it!'

'The flaming cheek of it! Peeping over our fence! I'll have to cut that damn creeping Ivy down near its roots, wait for it to die!' Harold whispered to Edith 'Just looking for my wife's contact lens!' Harold shouted, through the patio door.

'Thank you, Harold! Now I'll have to go about without my glasses!' Edith spat, contemplating life as a contact lens wearer.

During the following final weeks of summer, Harold and Edith got to know their new neighbours. Every time Edith pegged out the washing, she could hear the man shouting at his telephone, striding up and down his back garden 'Effing this and effing that'

The children turned out to be the least of her worries, it was the volume of their father's voice that was the problem... that man does not need a telephone. And to make matters worse, he popped his head over the fence. Again.

'You want to put some clothes on, love!'

Edith scurried inside and slid the patio door shut, almost catching the washing basket in the mechanism.

'That man! He just popped his head over the fence *AGAIN* and told me to put some clothes on!' Edith spied herself in the mirror, surely he could not have mistaken this peach coloured top for...? No!

Then came the issue with the wheelie bins. Like most suburban dwellers, Harold and Edith were obsessed with their bins. They routinely returned from the shops, on one particular bin day in September, but there was no sign of their emptied bins.

'You get on to the council, and I'll go and start the search!' Harold catastrophised. But no sooner had Edith been put through to 'please hold', Harold stomped back up the drive, dragging two bins behind him.

'The flamin' cheek of it! He tried to steal our wheelie bins!'

Later that same night, Harold and Edith's security light shone through their front door. The rolling sound of their wheelie bins taunted them. All they could do was lie there, security light dancing on their duvet, whilst being robbed of their waste disposal receptacles.

The following day, there was a loud knock on the door. Edith jumped out of her skin. She gingerly opened the porch door, the silhouette she saw behind the frosted glass was that of Mr Platt. She took off her spectacles (maintaining the illusion of a contact lens wearer) and opened the door.

'Just let me show you something in your back garden' He boomed.

'No! I mean, no! Is it about the Ivy plant? We know about it!'

'Just let me show you something!' One foot was on her porch step.

'No! Look! We killed the plant so that we could remove the fence!'

'Ohhhhh! So you killed the tree?' His arms were folded, his manner was condescending.

'We, well! It's not a tree, it's a plant' squeaked Edith, the mouse.

'Right, well it's getting a bit silly, isn't it? Sort it out, will you? ALRIGHT!'

'We already know! We are waiting for it to die off then...' Edith's voice died off just like the ivy ... Just because someone ends a sentence with 'alright' does not make it 'alright' Edith thought. When Harold returned from the newsagents, Edith was in a state. She told him all about the knock on the door.

'I just wish he would bog off, Harold!'

'Right, that does it! Enough's enough! I'm putting my foot down!'

Over the next few weeks, Harold plotted how to get rid of Mr Platt. He could not apply the same treatment he had given the previous neighbours. There could be no throwing dog dirt over the fence, no poisoning the cat, no blocking the cars in with his Morris Marina. Harold had to conjure and imagine utterly odious acts. After much agonising, he settled on a smear campaign...

Slander is a difficult crime to prove. The execution of such an act would involve the careful planting of gossip growing seeds, spreading malicious and fake statements about Mr Platt, including getting his name wrong 'Mr Pratt'.

Edith was no problem really, but Harold *was* doing this for her... with regret, Harold decided to employ Edith as the catalyst. He would have to take her down. Kill two birds at once, so to speak.

'Right, I'm off to my knitting circle, Harold. Don't forget to get that chicken out of the freezer'

'You be careful, Edith, I'm sure I saw our friend next door stood in his back garden *exposing* himself' Harold whispered the word 'exposing'.

'Oh... oh dear, well I can't wear my specs until I've passed their house anyway, thanks to your 'contact lens' stroke of genius! Right, see you later'

'Goodbye Edith,' Harold said, in cold tones. When she was out of sight, Harold flung the patio doors open, free to peruse his garden. But he felt like someone was watching him, that one shiny iris was following him right up to the hole in the fence. Harold stepped forward, a silent staring contest with his nightmare neighbour was soon realised. Oh! Does he know what my plans are? Did I say them out-loud? Harold rushed back inside. 'Oh! I forgot to get the chicken out!'...

The noise of the crashing fence shocked Harold. The wooden slats and the ivy plant were being thrown over the fence onto Harold and Edith's lawn! Total carnage!

'What the bloody hell!' Harold shouted out, from the safety of his kitchen.

When Edith returned from knitting, they had to haul the broken fence panels, splinters and all into the second rate wheelie bin (swapped by the neighbour a few weeks previously) Harold's plan was not going well, plus he realised there was no way of asking Edith if she had mentioned the 'flasher' next door at today's knitting group. He had not thought this through, it was just too suspicious to bring it into the conversation.

They ordered a new fence panel, of super strength plastic. This could neither be ruined by an overgrown Ivy or pushed over by an annoying neighbour. During the next few weeks, not always, but usually, if Edith was about to go out without Harold he would report some new misdemeanour from next door.

'He's been playing loud music' or 'He's been singing loudly... about *sex*' Harold's fibs got more and more desperate, and Edith became less and less interested. It took Harold until Autumn displayed the darkened days of Winter before he could invent another elaborate exaggeration.

'I'm sure I heard him doing a drug deal. Oh yes Edith, the devil has come to live next door. I heard him, effing this and effing that, arranging to take delivery, and this was going to make him rich! Rich I tell you!'

'Rich enough to move away I hope Harold. Oh, by the way, Edna's coming to stay next week. Henri doesn't like bonfire night so I said that she could stay. It might be quieter for them'

'Your sister! Well, 'spose she can answer the door on Halloween... Although, have you not been *listening*, Edith? I don't think it'll be quieter around here with those Pratt's next door. They've got *children* Edith, there's bound to be a *bonfire!*'

Harold's spectacles steamed up. His wife did not understand him, the plot against the new neighbour was a non-starter, and now his sister in law and her cat 'Henri-the-third' were coming to stay. Their arrival came all too soon.

'Helloooo! I am NOT getting deafened by whizz-bangers this year' Edna anticipated the perils of November.

'Don't worry, I'm in charge of all things firework-ey. You leave it to Harold'

He then launched into a story about why Catherine wheels are named Catherine wheels, getting it very wrong. Proving his theory by repeated assertion.

Harold and Edith went shopping, and he soon found what he was looking for amongst the 'super-buys '. Noise-cancelling headphones. He popped them into his rucksack. Harold had never been caught shoplifting in all his seventy-three years. When they arrived home, Harold accidentally (on purpose) let Henri out.

Harold settled down on the settee, ignoring the incessant meows, he nodded off. He thought he might have been dreaming, the meows graduated to purrs, something that a cat only does if being stroked by a human hand. Harold sat up. Someone was in the back garden! Again! He went to the patio window, but no one was there. Not even the cat.

Later that day, Edna realised her cat, Henri was missing. Harold confessed, and Edna berated;

'He's a house cat!' She sobbed. Henri-the-third was officially missing.

The third of November quickly became the fifth, and still, there was no sign of Henri.

'I'm going to look for him again. Edith, you stay here so there's a familiar face if he returns' said Edna, Harold opened his mouth to tell her how silly she was.

'Harold!'

'Yes?'

'Shut it!'Edna set off but did not get far on the slimy sediment leaf-covered path. Inside the house, Harold and Edith took it in turns (Harold first) to try on the noise cancelling headphones. They did not hear Edna's scream as she slipped, skidded, and fell headfirst into the door. There she lay, concussed under a pile of wet leaves. In the rain.

Edith had wondered what was in Harold's rucksack all their married life. He always had it with him, often forgetting how much space it occupied. Today it contained spare socks, breath freshener and a tin of peaches he was saving for later. He lifted his rucksack, swung it round his back and hit Edith clean in the face. The weight of it knocked her to the floor. Harold was still wearing the headphones, so did not hear the thump. And was not expecting her to be so close when he turned, tripped, and fell on top of his rucksack, and on top of Edith.

....

ARSON was not Mrs Platt's intention when she trespassed into Harold and Edith's back garden. Still, it was her fault, and therefore a crime all the same. She had heard all about her neighbour's missing cat at the knitting circle. That woman Edith had blatantly lied all those times, it was as though she was looking right through her. She ought to wear contact lenses or spectacles at least. There had been no answer when she had knocked on to return their cat, so she slid out the new plastic fence (with ease) to enable access to their patio window. The combination of her children's bonfire and her husband's illegal firework scam spilt flames all over her neighbour's lawn, the bungalow caught alight quickly... And now it was all over the papers.

TWO DEAD IN BONFIRE NIGHT DISASTER

Mr and Mrs Harold Sparrow died following a fire thought to have been started in a wheelie bin. A woman in her seventies found unconscious at the front door of the same address. One cat missing, presumed dead.

Mr Platt laughed to himself, he had always wanted a bigger garden.

Pogonophobia

'Grandma! Grandma! Look!' Kylie ran towards Grandma Shirley, waving yet another parent pressuring piece of paper. Shirley looked around the playground, it was home time and her granddaughter was often the first one out. Some of the other children, although not as excitable as Kylie, were also clutching copies of the same flyer.

'What is it, Kylie? Hmm? Stop jumping up and down! Do you need the toilet?' Shirley's arm was being pulled out of its socket. Either Kylie was getting strong for her age, or Shirley was becoming weak.

'It's the Christmas *fair,* Grandma! Father Christmas is coming!'

Grandma Shirley hid her groan.

The week flew by, as often they do at that time of year, and soon it was Saturday morning. Of course, chaperoning Kylie to the Christmas fair had fallen to the Grandparents. Try as they might, they could never refuse.

'I'm too tired for today really. There's always a lot of pushing and shoving, especially for that bottle tombola' Shirley confided in Keith.

'Shirley, are you sure it's not your... problem?'

'Don't mention it, Keith, please' cutting her husband's words off, Shirley started itching her face frantically.

'It does get worse at this time of year, Shirl, how long have we been married? I do notice these things you know' Keith was ever defending his title of 'most attentive husband'. 'I think I'm breaking out in spots now you've mentioned... you know... anyway, It's the standing about in queues, takes it out of me! I just want to stay at home with the heating on full, and relax with a nice E L James novel' crumpled Shirley.

'Don't worry, I've got just the thing, I found that foldaway stool when I was fetching the Christmas decorations. You can sit down and I will look after Kylie!' Keith had thought of everything.

Like a pile of presents, Kylie was ready to burst; she had been preparing list upon list to present to Father Christmas for a *very* long time. They made their way to the Christmas fair, it turned out that Keith had been right about the foldaway stool. Shirley looked with dread at the throngs of parents and children packing the school hall. She averted her eyes from the grotto.

'Right Grandma, you sit yourself down, and I'll take Kylie for a mince pie before we get in the grotto queue!' Keith whispered the word *'grotto'*

'Yeah Grandma, sit down!' Kylie ordered, agreeing with her Grandad.

'Well, I don't want to be in the way' Shirley sucked in a sharp anxious gasp.

'You won't be, don't worry'

So Shirley perched on her stool, watching her husband and Grandaughter get in the first of many queues. Kylie was jumping up and down like a Christmas bauble suspended from a plastic tree. At that moment, Shirley was glad they had brought her and glad she had brought the stool too. She was not sitting alone for too long, though.

'Hello, Shirley!' Their neighbour, Sue came over, then Linda the lollipop lady said hello and then Christine the librarian, who Shirley recognised from toddler's reading group.

'Hello, Shirley! I've missed you at the library!'

'Are you all set for Christmas? ... No, we're not either...' They chattered away. One of the women visited the mulled wine stall, and soon they were having a lovely time. Then Shirley noticed a man appear, he was standing next to Christine the librarian. He was wearing a hat indoors, a bright yellow T-shirt under his coat, he had extra long, greasy hair, and a vacant stare. Shirley could hardly bare look at him because he was also sporting a *beard!* Spidery course, fibrous threads jutting out the bottom half of his face. It was so unnatural. She drained her wine glass and adopted the coping strategy she used for anxiety provoking sights like these. Shirley squinted at the stranger with one eye. He was still standing there, how could he think he belonged in this circle of daytime drinking housewives? How could he think he belonged anywhere with that monstrosity on his face? Strangers with beards, Shirley's worst nightmare. Fear of beards is a recognised phobia. She risked a smile at him, but he did not smile back.

Who did he belong to?

'I see you've got your little friend with you?!'
Shirley whispered to Christine, who presumed
she meant her son, old enough to peruse the
Christmas fair alone. She had not noticed the
silent bearded stranger.
'Right girls, I'm off, I need to buy a ticket for
the bottle tombola! Even librarians like a
tipple at Christmas'
'See you, love, I'll start reading again now that
Kylie has started school, so I'll be seeing you!'
(Shirley didn't want to ask if they stocked
erotic fiction at the library)
Christine left the group of chattering women
which had now grown bigger, but the bearded
stranger did not follow her. Shirley looked
around the group of women. If he did not
belong to Christine, then who was he with?
Shirley's anxiety grew. Maybe her foldaway
stool had not been a good idea after all. She
nudged Linda, and whispered, 'Who's that
man with the beard?' Actually, she mouthed
the word 'beard', unable to bring herself to say
it.

Linda shrugged and carried on talking to Carol, the yoga teacher. More people had come into the school hall now, all paying fifty pence towards school funds. Shirley was getting a bit hot under the collar, she was sure the bearded stranger was moving closer to her... Then Keith rescued her with a cup of tea.

'I've just left Kylie in the face painting queue, Miss Duckworth's keeping an eye on her, but only for a minute'

'Well, look, look what's happened!' Shirley tried whispering to Keith, expecting him to protect her from the stranger.

'I've got to get back to her, Shirley, I'll be back in a minute!' Keith trotted off into the crowd. He really does need to try to be more observant. Shirley decided to take matters into her own hands.

'I'm just moving up a bit ladies, I don't want to be in the way!' Shirley shuffled her foldaway stool away from the bearded stranger. But he, in turn, with his facial hair, moved closer towards her: Shirley could not believe it! The more she moved away, the closer he got. She tried to get his attention, but he just looked ahead. She nudged Carol, and widened her eyes, nodding in his direction.

'Hello, love! Have you had too many goes on the bottle tombola?' Carol will stand for no messing.

No response... This fiasco had been going on for more than half an hour now, Shirley was going to have words with Melanie about all this extra babysitting...

Then She was distracted by Kylie running towards her.

'Grandma! I've been to see Father Christmas, and his *beard isn't real*! I pulled it and it made a snapping noise on his face! I think you'll be quite safe if you want to go and sit on his knee!' Kylie giggled, she threw herself at Grandma Shirley. They both fell off the stool laughing. When they opened their eyes, the bearded stranger had vanished. Shirley spotted him stood next to a new group of people, he had found someone else to follow, and torment with his untidy face prickles. Oh goodness! Shirley thought. He should not be hanging around inside a school, though, this is all very strange.

'Oh, Keith, look, that man I was telling you about has... Wait! Kylie! Don't go running off!'

Kylie ran towards the stranger, who, to Shirley's horror was talking to a little girl who looked to be Kylie's age.

'I'll go and see what's going on,' Keith said, whilst Shirley waited, hoping he wouldn't mention her phobia. She could not make out what was being said (partly because of the beard obscuring any chance of lip-reading) There was chatting and pointing, and then laughing. Kylie came skipping back over to Shirley.

'Grandma! Grandma! That man is not a stranger! He thought you were standing in a queue! He was saving a place for his little girl! Look! She is over there with her mummy, waiting for Father Christmas!' A woman waved at Shirley 'It's my friend from Miss Duckworth's class, Phoebe!'

Shirley and her friends laughed and laughed. And although Shirley was not quite ready for a trip to see the bearded Father Christmas, her close encounter with today's stranger may have softened her Pogonophobia.

V is For Very

Only September, but the wind nipped at my toes, my bare flesh, my nose. Same weather as it had been on that day, years ago. Can't believe that I can still feel the cold. Who knew?!
September, how it used to smell of newly sharpened pencils. That night I had the novelty of optimism, the perfect time when stars align. Could this be the one? The first flush of romance, a mobile beeps, a voice speaks That's how it was supposed to go. I should have told someone where I was going... I was exceptionally stupid.

Twenty-six was a funny age. Almost everyone I'd known had embraced one serious fling at least. I remember I'd been thinking, am I too young to settle down? It had been different for me, I had bought into the stereotype that 'all husbands cheat' ... I know I would have. And it wasn't as though I'd been 'one of the girls' from work, and I definitely wasn't like the blokes. Fleeting young men dressed in supermarket suits. Starting their careers in that oppressive office until promotion beckoned and they had moved on. Naturally, I'd always given them the once over but I'd always instantly known. Just like I had known from the very start what I was. Especially when I was a teenager; not so long ago. I'd been too old to be sitting there alone, I know. It wasn't like drinking cider in the park, in the dark with Cheryl and Lisa, I'd been their 'Gay best friend' but we'd lost touch. They might've been able to warn me, that Piccadilly Gardens is no place to meet a stranger.

'But I'm not a stranger' he had said 'You seem like a *very* nice boy'

What a creep! He'd paused at that point...

'Erm,' He laughed a smarmy laugh 'Now it's your turn to say something nice?... About me?'

I remember feeling patronised put down
y'know? But what do you say to something
like that? Lisa had been the same, come to
think of it, condescending cow ...
'Maybe it's just my sense of humour' he'd said,
to make me feel stupid, I presume.
Is this the way it goes then? I still don't know.
Why didn't I leave? I had sat down on that
bench, and I waited, of my own free will! I
arranged it! I've only got myself to blame,
entertaining an instant date on the internet and
expecting love at first sight. That's not how it
goes for people like me, and that's not all,
wait 'til I tell you... He was late! I thought he
was playing mind games, that's what I'd come
to expect. I'd continued sitting like a lemon. I
sat there! Sitting, waiting, missing,
despairing. Pulling, it happened more than
once, why did he pull my hair? Did no one
see that? A short half hour later, he would be
pushing me, pushing me into... Oh, I'll get to
that.
Desperate amongst the dirty drug dealing that
GMP had launched a crackdown on, I had
panicked, and shouted for help, like a stupid
little kid.

'But you don't need help' he had said 'You seem like a *very* dirty boy' I shuddered, yes I remember shuddering. Even my automatic nervous system had warned me he was dangerous, breathing into my neck, nipping at my bare flesh, even my nose.
'I can tell just by looking at you that...'
What he said next shall remain unsaid. I should have left... I could not leave. This is not the way it goes. A mobile beeps, a voice speaks my scream had broken up, cut off, I tried more than once. I could no longer reply.
'Look what you've done, this was your fault. This is all you deserve, you're a very filthy boy' he had hissed 'You've ruined my shirt with your mess' said a particularly smartly dressed urban legend serial killer.
I've gone. I met a psychopath. Walking away, holding me up, making out I was drunk for the CCTV. Drugged with legal highs until I died. Then he had the cheek to say:
'You weren't even worth it'
Soon, it will be someone else's turn.

Piccadilly Gardens is close enough to the canal, no one thought of that in the search. I don't remember much of that watery coffin. My DNA washed away, hypothermia concluded. Months later, only internet trolls respond to my 'Crimewatch' appeal. They only showed it once, Piccadilly Gardens is no place to be rescued.

Now I'm permanently here in the park, in the dark. I still can't believe I had been so naive. I mean, who goes on a date in the park? In Piccadilly Gardens FFS!

Time goes on, grief remains, I'm missed every second, of every day. The sun comes up and goes down again. Someone's sitting on me, on my bench, it's built to last, and stronger than it looks. Trust me, this happens all the time. 'Hey! Get off me!' He doesn't budge, you'll never guess.. oh no, I didn't mean! Don't worry it's not him back again, although I am on the lookout. I'm all prepared for what I would do, not revenge, just a simple case of making sure it doesn't happen again. The unwelcome guest is only the relentless roaring snoring of a neighbourhood tramp. How boring.

'Get your filthy hands off my previously shiny, engraved inscription' He can't hear me of course, but I managed to spook him. After a while, he tramps off to the all-night café. He isn't trapped like me, he can leave like I should've left. It's alright for some.

I'm sitting, waiting, warning on the memorial bench my mother insisted on. Although I don't really care for her chosen wording, she could have put more thought into it, found a few fancier words to describe my disappearance. V is for victim, not 'very' it sounds pathetic, listen:

Remembering Darren 22.6.80 -1.9.2006 *The day you disappeared. A very sad day.*

Pretty Scary

This is a true story. The names have not been changed to protect the innocent because this tale would be ruined by pseudonyms (and who needs protection?)
When I was in high school, I found something out about myself. It's not like I can tell you that *'I always knew I was different'* because I always knew that I'm just the same as the next hopeless wonder from the bowels of Bury. I always knew I was boring.
There was only one way of coping with this; open your bedroom window (later to become your car window) and treat your neighbours to the sound of Nevermind.
There is nothing better than listening to the band Nirvana. If you want me to get all music snobby about it, I'm talking about the grunge rock scene of Seattle from the early 90s. Exported to the UK and popular still today.
The very early 90s, because of Kurt Cobain...
I know I said I wasn't going to protect anyone, but we all know what happened.
I had just started my nurse training in April 1994, and I couldn't bear to listen to any music for at least a year after. It was pretty boring.

Life goes on. I did alright for myself in my career... I move house, my favourite cat dies, my daughter grows up. Then I meet my husband. We were always meant to be together, and before I knew it we were on the honeymoon of a lifetime in America. Today was our last day.

'I think we should go up to Aberdeen, see where Kurt Cobain grew up'

'I don't know if I feel right about it, It's like being nosy, won't it be scary?'

'I've only driven this hire car from the airport to the hotel all week! It's a waste!'

I agreed, we were already thinking of our credit card bills.

The weather reminded me of home, raining just like Manchester, the freeway hidden in fog and garnished either side with Douglas Fir trees. We drove and drove in silence because my iPod died during the first week of our holiday. I checked it was still there, safely drained and redundant in the front pocket of my handbag.

'Oh, sugar!' He slammed on the brakes... actually, he didn't say 'sugar' but you get the idea.

One $200 speeding ticket later, the last day of our honeymoon was not going well. The Grays Harbor traffic enforcement officer did not believe our story of tourism. Why would anyone want to come out here? An hour of careful driving later, and the sign cheered us:
'Aberdeen, 'Come As You Are'
Driving through this desolate town, poverty lived on every street, curtains hung limply in every window. Like a small dwelling place that had been hurriedly abandoned, because of a disaster, left just as it was.
'Oh, it feels so creepy! I wonder what Kurt Cobain would think of tourists visiting the place he grew up in? Be honest, it's only because he is *dead* that we are visiting' I could hardly bear to say the word 'dead' out loud just in case someone was listening.
'I know, look at the place, it's no wonder things turned out the way they did.' Husband said. Good job we were on our honeymoon, I would've killed him for that.
The town was completely flat, tiny one storey wooden bungalows, not a soul in sight. Advertising signs for bankrupt shops no fast food chains, no people. We parked up and got out to ask directions. It was like they had been watching us, the local homeless appeared like rattling skeletons.

'Do you have a dollar, sir? Can you spare a cigarette?'
I hid behind my husband.
'I think they think we're rich!'
That wasn't the worst of it... A pair of teenagers appeared on BMX bikes sweeping in and out of cars on the road and pavements. 'This is it, we're going to die, they're gonna mug and murder us, this is how it's gonna end, and it's only just begun'
But they meant us no harm, they just wanted to look at the car. I told you this was a true story. We asked them if they went to the same school, as Kurt Cobain had.
'Who?' They didn't even know who he was
'Say somethin' else in your accent, man!'
I couldn't think of anything to say, although later I wondered if they had ever thrown the windows open, and turned the music up loud. In their town without sound.
'You should go to the seafood restaurant further down the river,' The other teenager said.
'No, it's closed down, don't you remember? It burnt down, and one hundred people had to jump into the water, some of them drowned'
'Yeah, but it's reopened'
'I don't think it has!'
'I work there near there!'

We left them arguing at the side of the road, found the memorial park at the stump of a dead end street. Nothing to show really just a lonely concrete guitar mounted in the middle of a tiny piece of grass at the side of the road. Not a museum with a gift shop, like every other place of interest in America. We were the only sorry visitors that day. We found Kurt Cobain's Mother's house, his ghostly childhood home, complete with 'for sale' sign, took some photographs, was someone twitching the curtains? Quick! Get in the car! And that was that.

'I feel spooked out, it's like we're being watched. Let's go back' I had goose-bumps, I thought that only happened in Stephen King novels.

'I'm hungry, I want to find that seafood place' Husband is always hungry.

We followed the BMX boy's directions, and sure enough found it. A burnt block of cinders should have been demolished but instead, right next to it a new building, a newly opened seafood restaurant mocking the tragedy, but fortunately closed on Tuesday evenings.

'We don't belong here!' I cried, as we were stared away from the second restaurant we tried, face to face with the small minded attitude that Kurt Cobain had written about. The flashy white car, our week of fake wealth joined the freeway for the last time, heading for the Seattle hotel that suddenly felt like home.

'What's that noise?' I heard a tinny sound in the front of my handbag 'It sounds like ... No, it can't be!' I stared in disbelief and wonder, my dead iPod had defied physics and magically switched itself back on! We found out what Kurt Cobain thought of our visit because the sound was the sound of Nirvana. Telling me my tourism wasn't a mistake, from the other side. I wasn't boring and I wasn't being stupid.

Plenty has been said and written about Nirvana frontman Kurt Cobain, but if you want to know anything about him, all you need to do is visit Aberdeen, Washington state, USA. It's pretty scary.

One Small Step

'Holidays are the best week of the year! Better than Christmas or my birthday!' Bobby announced. His baby sister, Sophie was too young to pick a favourite week, because every week is a favourite week when you are twenty months old.

'Where are we going this year Daddy?'

'Can you guess Bobby? It's a town by the sea beginning with 'B'!' Ben loved coastal resorts, visiting Blackpool and Bognor Regis in recent years.

'Are we going to towns beginning with 'B' because of our names? Ben and Bobby? What about 'D' for Daddy?'

'Yes Ben, what about 'S' for Sue and Sophie? Are Skegness or Southport ever going to get a turn?' Sue teased her husband before he had a chance to answer their son.

'No! We're going to Brighton because it has an amusement arcade on the pier!' Ben put Bobby on his knee.

'Fair enough! I suppose Sophie is too little to pick our holiday destination just yet, but in a few years we can gang up on you two and go to all the places that begin with 'S'! Spain for one!' Sue picked up Sophie's gurgling baby monitor.

'Don't worry, son there is a place in Spain called Barcelona, and, as you know, that begins with a 'B'!' Ben winked at Bobby, and they snuggled up on the settee.

Most boys develop a fixation for a hobby. Before Ben grew up and married Sue, he was fixated on aliens. His parents had blamed Doctor Who. The BBC had been at it again, putting ideas into a young boy's head. What Ben's parents did not realise, however, is that they were to blame. Had they not have banned Ben's fixation on a life imagined beyond the stars, then he would not have been so interested. His mother had to do the shopping and do the ironing. His Dad had to go to work and go to the pub. By the time Ben got into Star Trek, little green men were just getting in the way. Hard to believe then, that Ben should become a man and meet Sue, but they started dating just around the time when geeks became fashionable. Unfortunately, Sue's only memory of Doctor Who was one of hiding behind the settee. Too scared to glance at the alien enemy portrayed by the BBC. But they got to know each other and fell in love. A wedding and two children later, Ben and Sue knew one another very well. Ben was not a big drinker, but Sue always knew when he was one Jack Daniels and coke away from talking about aliens. Their son Bobby was of an impressionable age. About to select his first hobby, his first childhood interest that would grow memories never forgotten. Ben was forbidden by Sue from talking about aliens.

First Bobby started collecting action figures, then it was football stickers, but when his little sister Sophie was born, Bobby started taking photographs... He was given his mum's old mobile phone, taking pictures in black and white, sepia and panoramic. His eighth birthday present was a digital camera, photographs of his sister, his parents, his grandparents, their house, the goldfish, all lovingly captured by little Bobby. The camera was taken everywhere, snapping moments with its one seeing eye close to the ground, soon his sights were set on becoming a professional photographer. His snapshot treasures will be valued for years to come. Although sometimes, the sight of Bobby with the camera in situ on his face and those unflattering early morning shots started to grate on Sue's nerves.

'BOBBY!' Sue immediately regretted shouting at her son, in fairness, however, she was panda-eyed and had Sophie's breakfast down her front.

'Be careful, Bobby! People need a warning before having their photo taken... You have to get their permission! Would you like it if I took your photo when you weren't expecting it?' Ben stepped in.

The shock of both parents chastising Bobby made his little cheeks bright red. 'They'll be sorry when I'm a famous photographer!' He folded his little arms and stuck out his bottom lip.

Driving to Brighton was fairly uneventful. Sophie encapsulated and asleep in an industrial strength car seat. Bobby secretly snapping scenery out of the car window. A girl in a car at the side of theirs pulled her tongue out at him. He did not take her photo, he did not have her permission.

'First one to see the sea gets five points!' Said Ben.

During the holiday, the family enjoyed the delights of Brighton. Including leisure facilities and franchise eateries that could be found anywhere, but soon became favourites. The pier (for amusements and doughnuts) the sunshine (not guaranteed, but gratefully accepted) And best of all the beach. Their picnic blanket bobbled over the cobbles and stones. Hot in the day, and cool at night.

'Ice creams for everyone!' Said Ben. Bobby took several photographs of Sophie wearing hers and laughing. Frisbee games and paddling, more photos taken. The weather was kind to Ben, Sue and their children.

'Good choice, husband, the shingle beach is less sand and mess between the toes!' Sue swooned at Ben, her priorities changed by motherhood.

'And the sun has brought out your freckles' Ben gently kissed Sue, his admiration unchanged since the day they met.

'Time to go back to the hotel, Bobby!' Once Sophie was safely strapped in the stroller, Bobby's shutter snapping started up again.

'One more picture! One more photo! I've got to practice for when I'm famous!'

'One step at a time, Bobby! You can't expect to be famous straight away!' Ben tried to lift Bobby onto his shoulders, realising today was the day that his son had grown too heavy to be carried.

'I don't need picking up, Daddy! I'm taking small steps! Look!' Bobby tiptoed up the steep hill back to the hotel, whilst taking photographs.

'You can upload them as soon as we get home' Ben promised an excited Bobby.

Sue put Sophie to bed for the last night in the Hotel.

Bobby sat in between his parents on the double bed, and of course, they had to look at today's photographs. The beach, the pier, Sophie's face full of ice-cream. Ben's nostrils. Sue's muffin top stomach. Towards the end of the photographs, something caught Ben's eye. An image, alien to what he was expecting to see. An image he had been forbidden to see. As he zoomed in on the last photograph, his mind flooded with memories of men on mars and American conspiracies. When Ben's eyes focused on the dark crevices of the shingle stones, a pair of eyes peeped up at him, he shouted out something that he had wanted to say for the last ten years:

'WE ARE NOT ALONE!'

'Give it to me! Let me look!' Bobby and Sue inspected the screen, they could not quite make out what was underneath the stones.

'What can you see?' Bobby excited by his dad's revelation.

'Look under these stones' Ben pointed 'They look like two eyes, peeping out! It's an alien! It's obviously an alien!'

'Don't be silly! It's probably a crab! Do they live on shingle beaches, though?' Sue said.

'No, they do not live on shingle beaches! Well, I don't think so anyway, how would they survive? No! It's definitely an alien. You should send that photograph off somewhere, son you've probably discovered something!'

Ben's alien talk cork had popped, and he had plenty to say. Bobby had never seen this side of his daddy before and gaped in awe at him. Maybe he had eaten too many green lollies...

Sue stepped in, like the voice of reason.

'Well I don't know about that, but at least we know what you're going to be, Bobby, when you step out into the world!'

'What's that Mummy?'

'A famous photographer, of course!'

Bobby's heart burst with his parent's encouragement.

Back on the beach, and out of its depth, a little two-eyed creature from outer space crouched underneath the shingle stones. looking both ways, to make sure it was safe, it took one small step out into the world.

And she was not alone...

The Witch Hunt

Hatred and hysterical fear had proved to be a powerful tool for Alec S Hopkins. Suited, booted, quiff sculpted. Self-promoted to the legal side of things within the city council. A civil litigator. A cost cutting position invented by the local housing association. Alec was paid slightly higher than the minimum wage to extinguish anti-social and nuisance tenants. Listening, and taking the side of the judgemental majority in the neighbourhood. Putting together paper-thin cases on paper-thin paper. He would then forward these by e-mail to a recipient he knew would be unable to answer. He also knew that no response to his correspondence would be a lever he could use against the tenant in a court of law. Catapulting a case, fuelled by prejudicial petitioners.

This is a convoluted way of explaining how Alec S Hopkins employed tricks and shenanigans to achieve results in his line of work, as the hatchet man of the housing association.

Fear, anxiety and general paranoia had proven crippling and soul destroying for Tina Dodds. She lived in the wrong place, at the wrong time. Her only crime was her slovenly nature. Seen locally as a 'bit of a nuisance', today she was wearing a tracksuit and trainers and she was sitting in her flat in the cold, alone. The damp smell of stale nicotine permeated her hair, her skin, her being. She was rolling herself a paper thin fag, with a paper thin rolling skin. In the dark. She considered if she should answer the door to a woman who visits her every so often. This woman, who had just tampered with the doorbell rattled the letter box and rapped her knuckles against the window in a loud and bossy fashion. The sound of the visitor had broken the silence, Tina had jumped out of her skin and then sat back down again. She licked the long edge of the paper and methodically rolled the tobacco in her fingers. She could not, for the life of her remember the name of this woman, who was standing on the other side of her paper thin door. She was not coming round for a chat, and yet she was now holding open Tina's letterbox and shouting conversations at right at her.

'Open the door love! I need to find out how you've been!'

She only seemed to come around when the block was noisy, or there had been increased bother and nuisance. If Tina heard lots of loud whispering, then this woman would magically appear. Joking, once that she only calls around when it is a full moon! She should not joke about the moon, this woman, the silly fool. No, she only appeared when things got 'noisy'. And her fingertips were now protruding through Tina's letter box.

'Hello, love! It's me, Beverley. I've been trying to get hold of you for three weeks, you're late love!'

Beverley! That's her name! Tina's mouth dried, her heart thumped inside her thin, weedy frame, she felt dizzy when she stood, she opened the door and when she recognised Beverley's face, memories flooded back. Memories of sitting and listening to a softly spoken Irish man. He sounded so gentle, that Tina would have agreed to anything. He sounded so gentle, that Tina was not really listening to anything. During that appointment, she had been sure that she could hear her neighbours whispering through the walls.

'Ye old crone! Witch! Have you made a pact with the devil? Did he mark you? Did you have sex with the devil?'

What had her neighbours been doing in that mental health centre anyway? The walls must have been paper thin, Tina remembered she could hear everything they were saying. Just like in her flat... The walls are paper thin there too. Her flat, she remembered she was still there, in her flat, this woman's voice dragging her back to reality.

'Ok love, are you ready?' Beverley was holding up one of those needles that women like her carry about with them. Tina felt a sharp scratch in her behind, this what she must have eventually agreed to with that softly spoken doctor, even though she could not listen properly, because of the voices. Tina pulled up her tracksuit bottoms, and Beverley left. Tina returned to rolling her paper thin cigarette. Amongst the chaos of her flat, she noticed that Beverley had forgotten the hypodermic syringe, it was sticking out of the arm of her sofa. 'And they say I'm dirty!' Tina spoke to herself. Beverley and her needle had upset Tina's equilibrium, set her mind racing. Now, what was she trying to think of? Her mind was foggy, her thoughts disordered. Had Beverley said something about medication? She scratched her head and examined her dirty fingernails. Yes, she had! That woman had accused Tina of not taking her medication! The cheeky cow! What does she know about my tablets?! They're wrong anyway I can look after myself! Tina turned her flat upside down looking for the 'venalink' card, it should be full of psychotropic drugs, an A4 sized piece of card with the days of the past few weeks written on it (for those in need of compliance) She had found it, ha! Proof!

But now all her belongings were scattered over the floor, including the contents of her ashtray. Tina thought about tidying up. She thought about how she could not remember what she was supposed to be thinking about. Her mind was playing tricks on her, Tina's thoughts had been stolen from her... The dirty buggers! Stealing her thoughts through these paper thin walls!

Her cat padded its paws over the sea of paper, an ashtray and its own litter. Tina remembered watching something on TV in the old days about cats. Apparently, they will only inhabit a place if it is 'fastidiously tidy'. Meaning her flat must not be that bad after all... Proof for all those nosy buggers who think I am 'unclean' she thought. Ha!...Her eyes were drawn to the sofa, her thoughts turned again to Beverley, the lazy unprofessional nurse who had a habit of leaving hypodermic syringes puncturing patient's furniture. Tina quickly opened her front door and neatly placed the syringe on her front doorstep. A used syringe for all to see glinting in the light of the communal landing. Satisfied that she had made her home safe to share with her cat and that she would not be disturbed, should Beverley return for the syringe. Tina decided to catch up on her sleep. She smoothed down the backside of her tracksuit bottoms, they were getting threadbare. The cheap material was paper thin. She curled up on her hallway floor, by her front door.

It was the noise that woke her. A whispering sound. At first, Tina had thought she was dreaming it. But then the whispers got louder and louder. She stood up in her hall at her front door. The noise that had woken her sharp in her ears a message just for her. Chanting, questioning, judging.

'When did you make a pact with a demon? Did you have sex with him? Did he dint you?'

'Who's there? ' Tina shouted. She stood up and tried the light switch. No electric again. 'Beverley? Is that you? Did you steal my leccy card?' Tina tried to remember if it was dark before the nurse called around. The noise has stopped... When Tina shouted out, the voices ceased... She stood up in the dark and cold, a draught blowing through her letterbox. Dare she look if someone has left the communal front door open again?

Tina's heart was rattling in her chest, her mouth tasted like an ashtray. She felt her way along the hall and found her bathroom. She pulled down her pants and sat down, relieved and held on to her tracksuit tightly whilst she sat there. 'Witch! Witch! Witch!' they were shouting at her again! Waiting for her to use the toilet! Tina's eyes darted about in the dark. 'Where are you?' The voices sounded like they were coming from next door. They sounded like they were in the walls of her flat. The paper thin walls! The dirty buggers! She flushed the loo. The ancient plumbing rattled through the entire building. Nowhere to hide, her fear turned to hate. 'Where are you? You dirty buggers! You woke me up!' She made her way down her hall, only the streetlights illuminating the inside through her paper thin curtains. Tina punched her walls 'Where are you? You dirty gets!' she shouted.

'Witch! Witch! Witch!' the voices answered. Her knuckles were bleeding. She wiped her hands on her face. Reaching her front room, she continued with her prior hunt through her belongings. This time looking for a flat surface to rest on. Six and a half hours after that woman, Beverley's visit, Tina fell back to sleep on her front room chair.

'Witch! Witch! Witch!' getting fainter and less accusatory.

The following day, Alec S Hopkins was reading the latest email correspondence from that particular block of flats. The prejudicial petitioners had been in communication with him again, and Alec was lapping it up. 'Noise at all hours, banging that sounded like someone fighting with their own internal walls. As if they were paper thin! A hypodermic syringe left out on the front doorstep for all to see! I can only presume that this has been used for illegal drug use! She's a nuisance, and we want her out' Alec S Hopkins gathered his one-sided information. He drafted a letter and posted it to Tina. This was the first course of action when dealing with nuisance and anti-social behaviour. A letter requesting that a meeting takes place, to discuss and remind Tina of her tenancy agreement. A letter in a brown envelope designed to strike fear into the heart of its recipient. A letter that was sure to cause anxiety and sleep deprivation. The closest thing to torture that Alec could wish upon Tina, the nuisance tenant. This legal threat, this method was employed by ruthless civil litigators, too stupid to read their own guidelines correctly.

Tina Dodds had been born in the wrong place at the wrong time. She had received brown envelopes through the post before and always they had caused anxiety and insomnia. This brown envelope was no different to the others and would stay unopened on the floor of Tina's hallway. Along with letters from the department of work and pensions and appointment cards for the local mental health treatment centre. As long as the letter remained unopened, Tina would be unaware of its implications, but the brown windowed envelope carried a veiled threat. She knew it was an official letter. This declaration of uncertainty was a means of torture. She could not open the letter. Tina Dodds knew what was coming. She had heard those threats through the paper thin walls. The noise had kept her awake at night. For a week she had not slept because of the noise from that letter, this most recent brown envelope had stopped her from sleeping. Wherever she laid down her head in that stale damp paper thin flat, she could hear the noise of the letter.

'We know what ye hast don, We're sick of ye noise, get out! Absquatulate! Ye cantankerous weaker vessel!'

Over the next few weeks, she could not sleep she could not smoke she could not eat. She still could open that envelope. Tina had no routine, void of habits a shell, a shadow of her former self in her paper thin cheap decorative garments. Experiences swimming around the cauldron of her head like a word salad. Things are often different during the night. What some call the witching hour, by those with moral panic. The temperature had changed. Winter was here. Winter had brought the Supermoon which was feared by the residents of Tina's block. The first thing that happened, (whatever time it was) was the heavy metal door blowing open and there ensued a superior figure in a long black coat. Her hair pointed and black sculpted onto her superior skull. She had a means of getting in and did not need to shock Tina into opening the door. One minute she was there with the breeze at the communal door, the next she was inside Tina's flat wishing away with one glance the stale ashtrays, the cat litter and the rotting cat food. The horrific state of things, the smelly version of Tina banished away. 'Tina! Tina! Get up from there. Come on, get changed let's sort things out'

Tina stood up like she was in a dream and methodically obeyed. She attended to her hygiene as though she had never forgotten how. She found clean clothes she stepped out of the shower into the light. She was under the spell. The flat transformed, the thin curtains opened, order was found. This moon came around but once a year and not for a chat. Once a year was enough to appear at the time that things were getting noisy. When brown envelopes collected and Tina could not cope. 'Now then Sister, I know what has been troubling you. I will open this brown envelope. It's paper thin. What harm can it do?'

In a trance, Tina obeyed. Her sister read for herself the threats and the chants. She threw back her head and laughed a superior laugh. 'I know what he's up to, I know what he's done! A bunch of clowns! A moral panic! Alec S Hopkins when did *you* make a pact with the devil? A crude plan! Your card is marked from this day on, you can be sure of that you witch hunter's son!'

The same wind blew out the superior figure with her long black coat. Tina Dodds curled up with her cat 'Goodbye Nats!' she cooed as she fell into a sleep she had been waiting for all week.

The second thing that happened (whatever the time was) is as follows: Beverley had remained tight-lipped over Tina Dodds' well-being. Alec S Hopkins had continued to bully her, with correspondence she was not in a position to answer for reasons of conduct and confidentiality. The last letter instructed she should attend the proposed meeting, whereby Alec S Hopkins would read the riot act, the tenancy agreement to Tina Dodds. And therefore expedite her eviction. Alec had requested Beverley's view, prior to the meeting asking if Tina Dodds has 'capacity'? Would Tina understand what was being said to her? Alec S Hopkins had misguidedly quoted the mental capacity act. Clever incorrect use of the wrong law. He also wanted Beverley there, 'in case Tina becomes difficult or violent'. Beverley scoffed at Alec's lay man's view... so judgemental. Even if she could explain to Alec S Hopkins, she would not be able to get him to understand. Tina Dodds is frightened of everything! Even brown envelopes! Why do you have to be so discriminatory? Beverley rolled her eyes. She pencilled the meeting into her diary and tried to telephone Tina on one of the many mobile phone SIM card numbers she had provided. The pencil marks in Beverley's diary disappeared as soon as she shut it.

Tina would not have heard the mobile phone ringing anyway. She was enjoying a peaceful sleep. Still under her sister's charm, from the previous night's visitation. No noise, no mess, no fear.

Alec S Hopkins admired himself in the mirror in his office, at the local authority housing association. Suited, booted, quiff sculpted. A black shadow appeared briefly in the corner of the mirror and then disappeared. Must have been Fiona, the woman he has to share an office with.

'Oi! You'll crack that mirror one day, you poser!' Fiona's loud voice bombarded Alec through the open window. Fiona was shouting at him from the car park and was not in the room at all. Alec froze and looked around, but he was alone. The morning hum of computers. The faint ringing of telephones downstairs. Not wanting to admit he was too scared to look back in the mirror, he stood in front of the window, ready to give Fiona a two fingered salute. Professional was he. Fiona shook her head and walked into the office building. Behind her, Alec S Hopkins observed a dark figure, a striking superior figure in a long black coat striding across the gated car park.

She only did things like this when life was getting out of hand. Her sister's fragility was wearing paper thin. She had a means of entrance and did not wish to shock the administrator on the front desk. She filled the reception area with the smell of patchouli. 'Excuse me,' She said 'I found this in your car park, on the floor, please ensure it reaches the man to whom it is addressed' Sliding the internal manilla envelope towards the woman, who in a trance said something she would repeat a thousand times in previous weeks. 'What name shall I give?'
'What name you ask? I simply found this letter, and if you could be so kind. But if you insist that a name is required, please tell him 'Love from Nat Ash, kiss kiss' She turned around and strode from where she came. The administrator scurried upstairs with that one letter and spoke in a way she had never spoken before
'Alec S Hopkins, I must be true and I must be quick.
This letter here is someone's wish
to reach you, but I must not snitch.
The messenger she looked like a .....'
The word the administrator wanted to say was on the tip of her tongue, but she could no longer speak. She ran coughing out of the office as if her mouth was filled with feathers.

Fiona appeared to shake her head, turned her own computer on and got on with her work. Alec opened the envelope. The smell of incense blew into the office. The paper that came out of the envelope curled up on his desk. Held together by what looked like a black hair elastic.

'Know this Alec S Hopkins and know your place. You are a clown, a huge disgrace. Continue to torture my sister and your true colours will be revealed upon your face'

'Right, I'm just going back downstairs to get the post. Are you alright love? You look a bit peaky' Fiona said to Alec S Hopkins, a confused man.

'Why don't you get thingy- me- jig to bring it? You know the woman who just came in here and started coughing? You know, the woman who works at the front desk?'

'I don't know what you're talking about, we haven't had a receptionist since the cuts came in. You want to try taking more water with it, Alec! Done me backside good though up and down these stairs!' Fiona said, patting her own bottom as she left the office. No this is not right, Alec S Hopkins was sure he had seen a woman giving him a message. Fiona was sat right there! He refused to move until Fiona returned. When she did, she put on his desk the internal envelope he thought he had already opened. The curled up paper with the strange incantation disappeared. He looked around. Fiona was acting like her normal self, eating her cereal bar and playing solitaire on the computer. Her stupidity did not sooth him. His letter was a summons to the annual mandatory training. This horrific annual demand by the housing association was now going to be a two-day event. Half way down the page, the reason for the extension was explained.

'It has come to the attention of the local authority, that the mental capacity act is being misused and misquoted when dealing with our vulnerable tenants. We are also including a longer version of the equality and diversity training'

Over the next few days, life started to change for Tina Dodds. In her newly clean flat. The walls did not appear so paper thin. No further letters arrived. The date of the meeting with Alec S Hopkins and Beverley was safely kept in her sister's long coat pocket. Tina also dared to leave her flat during the day. She only went to the local shop, but everything seemed different. She noticed the clouds in the sky. The sound of the traffic. She noticed a passer-by smiling at her. She could not hear any unwelcome noises. She did not even think about her neighbours. As she approached the communal door, it opened and a hook-nosed old woman stepped out with her trolley bag. Tina said hello to the stooped lady, who said 'hello' back.

Over the next few days, life started to change for Alec S Hopkins. The first day he caught a glimpse of himself in the office mirror. He was sure he had seen a dark shadow in the corner, he tried not to look at it. However, a protruding lock of red curls caught his eye. Alec stood up with a start and let out a scream when he looked at himself in the office mirror. He pulled at the bright red curls bouncing from his head. They had replaced the polished quiff that Alec had adopted for years to hide and manage his natural hair. He pulled at it. How did it get so long? Fiona looked up from her desk, and then down again. Alec had been acting strangely since yesterday. Turned his office desk upside down looking for a mysterious letter that no one else had seen. Alec reached into his desk drawer and being the type of man to have a manicure set in his office drawers, he pulled out a pair of nail scissors. He looked over at Fiona, who raised one eyebrow at him. Why has she not said anything about my hair? This is a nightmare! Alec stood there in the mirror, tugging and hacking at his deep red wiry curls. He tried to dampen them down with water. He had water running down his face and bright orange curls bristling on his head. He kept hacking and cutting, as one orange tendril dropped onto the floor, another would grow and replace it. Fiona started laughing at him.

'Are you joking! What are you doing?!' Fiona had never dealt with this kind of situation before, it was a shock to see one of her work colleagues cutting his own hair.

'There's a hairdresser over the road if you're that desperate!'

Alec ran from the office. Down the stairs. He turned to the woman on the front desk, intending to give instructions about how long he would be. Fiona had been right, there was not a soul sat at the front desk. He strode over to the hairdressers 'Please, cut it all off!' Alec pleaded. It did not take long. Soon Alec was back to his old self. Smart and slick. He went back to the office, large sunglasses made his head look like a human fly. He stepped through the door and was sure he got a knowing nod from the woman on the front desk. He whipped his sunglasses off with one hand, looked up and saw again that he was alone in the reception, the woman had disappeared. When he got to his office door, his hand stroked the back of his head and he realised the hairdresser had not cut it as short as he had asked for. He stepped in and Fiona dropped her packet of crisps. Her mouth was wide open.

'Going for a new look? It's about time! Right, I'm off now. Meeting at the town hall. See you later'

The following day, Alec put his suit on, did up his boots, and then took them off again. It felt like he had something in his shoe. His hair was coarse and more difficult to comb into his usual quiff. He went about his business, but by lunch time he had rubbed a hole in the big toe of his sock on his left foot. At the end of the day, he looked in the mirror again. His hair had returned to the orange monstrous wig he had tried to get rid of yesterday... The next day, he struggled to put his boots on. He had worn a hole in both socks with his toes. It was the day he had arranged to go and visit Tina Dodds with her community nurse, Beverley. His toes were painfully pinching in his boots. He telephoned Beverley's office and was told that she had taken the day off because she thought her diary was clear! Alec brushed his hand against his hair. Of course! It was growing back thick and fast. The weekend started and Alec was soon to disappear, he had no choice, but to hide away. He thought he saw his neighbours sniggering at him, as he made his way, crawling from his car to the communal door of his apartment. When he prized his boots off, his toes were bleeding. Growing toe knuckles imprisoned by his smart boots. He soaked his feet in a bucket of warm water, which in turn, his right foot became wedged into and he stumbled around his apartment as though he was part of a terrible comedy sketch. Alec S Hopkins cancelled a date he had been looking forward to and was now in solitary confinement. He watched box sets of American crime dramas. The stories all merged into one, he was losing his ability to concentrate, continuing to watch, square eyed, in a trance. The weekend had started and disappeared again. By Monday morning, all that Alec could fit on his feet were a pair of red corduroy slippers his mother bought him for Christmas. Two sizes too big. Over the weekend, Alec had stopped looking in the mirror. He had not posted a single selfie on social media. He shuffled, bow-legged into his office. Fiona was sat there, as usual, eating crisps, and emptying her hole punch into the standard issue waste paper basket.

'I like your slippers, Alec!'

'They were all I could fit on my feet! They'll understand in court won't they?'

....

Today was the day pencilled in Alec's diary to apply to the courts to start eviction proceedings for Tina Dodds. His case was paper thin, his feet were dressed in bedroom wear, his hair was uncontrollable. He accidentally caught his reflection in a mirrored door... his nose was bright red! A weekend of indoor activities, festering in his pyjamas watching hours of television and drinking wine. Alone. The pizza delivery boy had sneezed right in his face. His immune system could not cope, and now his nose was bright red.

'Look at me! For God's sake look at me, Fiona! I'm a shadow of my former self! Look at my hair! Look at my feet!'

'Your hair has always looked like that! And you've been mincing around like your boots and trousers are too tight for as long as I have worked with you!' Fiona picked up the waste paper basket 'Here! Catch!' The contents of the bin, from Fiona's hole punch fluttered all over Alec.

'Wait! What do you mean? I've always looked like this? My hair is inexplicable'

'Yes Alec, it is, but it has always looked like that '

Alec patted his hair, the horror, the disbelief. 'This is like a bad dream'

'Look I'll show you' Fiona pulled a pile of post out of her desk drawer. The type of nonsense women hold on to 'See, housing association of the year award, there's me stood next to the mayor who presented the award, and who is he stood next to? Oh yes! You! With your mass of orange curls. Last year's Christmas party, here is me in my new Christmas dress. Sat next to you, look' Alec did look, a mass of orange curls was escaping from a paper thin party hat.

'No! It can't be! This is a nightmare! I look like a... ' Horrified, he looked up at Fiona and looked at himself in the mirror 'I look like a clown!' Alec S Hopkins looked at his own identification badge and a red curly wig and red nose shone back up at him.

'You do... and today you look like a sad clown. Careful you don't get arrested!' Fiona left the room. She left him alone with the shadow in the corner, reminding him of the day when he saw that figure striding across the car park. The promise in the first letter that 'true colours will be shown upon his face'. He could not go to court on that day, he would have to adopt another way, try to understand Tina's difficulties and put a plan in place. Not just Tina, though, all his vulnerable tenants. He would have to pay attention to the mandatory training day. The self-promoted fool.

Tina Dodds held the communal door open for one of her elderly neighbours, the hook-nosed lady with a big chin looked up and said 'Thanks, Love' Maybe she had imagined the shouting through the paper thin walls? What had she been accused of? Tina should have written this down, on paper thin paper, she could no longer recall her voices. She went to see Beverley and the softly spoken doctor. 'I thought they were hunting me down, saying I was a witch. But I think I'm alright now'

The Storm In A Teacup

It had been raining for days. A 'storm', they had said so on the news. A disturbed state of the astronomical atmosphere. Wind, hail, rain, a rabbit's hutch blown away. A cyclone in June! The endless storms had caused severe disruption across the U.K. Flooding, pubs destroyed, power cuts in Radcliffe. Flags cracked by lightning outside Jane's house, and today she had a dentist appointment.

When she was a young woman, Jane had romanticised about a suitor sweeping her off her feet, she dreamt he would surprise her with a surging whirlwind of love. This tall, charming Romeo would knock at her parent's front door, for no other reason than to single Jane out and rescue her from her perceived confines.

'Jane, I know we have only just met, but I'm gorgeous, can I take you out?'

She imagined her hero taking her as his wife, fairly soon after that first cup of tea, and loving her so much that he would spend all his money on her. Just enough money to keep her in nice clothes, she would not be greedy, but in this imagined life, she would live a life of luxury and never have to work...

And she would never, ever have to step into a deceptively deep puddle, as she had done today, on this weather weary morning. The puddle had made her feel sad. The puddle immersing her right leg in rainwater up to her knee reminding her of the imaginary hero. The suitor, who had never materialised. She was in her forties now. Shy, adorable, a 'people pleaser'. Jane was so nice that people often took advantage without Jane realising. She had been manipulated by 'users' borrowing money from her. At work, she tried and tried to charm her colleagues. She baked, she paid double tea and coffee fund money, she took the draughty desk by the door, they repaid Jane by pushing their own workloads on to her, assuming she would not mind, because she was 'nice'. She had got used to this way of existing and had no meaningful relationships, hobbies or interests of her own.

Today was not going well for Jane, first, she had stood in a puddle, now, she was worried about being late, especially as dentist appointments often elongate. When she finally escaped the dentist's drill, it was still raining. She shut herself inside the safety of her car and sped off to work, the sun was starting to creep out from behind the grey clouds. Janet hated being late and was already anticipating the hard time that Paula from the front desk was about to give her. She was not one for motorway driving, but today she was in a rush. By now, the morning congestion had drained away. Tarmac shone in front of her like stretched black leather. She had no need for the fast lane, she was leaving at the next junction. The rain had started again, she hesitated to turn her windscreen wipers on because she had spotted something... a yellow plastic envelope shoved under the left wiper. The same shiny colour of yellow as a child's painting. It was the same yellow as ... NO! 'A parking ticket?' Jane's heart thumped in her chest 'This has *never* happened to me before!'

In sheer panic, she turned the windscreen wipers on. The new batch of rain wiped away, along with the yellow plastic envelope, fluttering away on the breeze, lost forever... lost, like the dreams she had of meeting her whirlwind romance hero. Lost, and out of Jane's field of vision, the plastic envelope was heading straight for the windscreen of the car behind her. Jane's initial reaction was to get out and try to retrieve the parking ticket, her car was now approaching the set of traffic lights at the junction of the motorway turn off. In her flustered state, she put the wipers on full pelt, beeped her horn by accident, and stalled her car. What should Jane do? She was not able to drive the wrong way down the motorway slip road, and she did not have the time to go back to where her journey had started so that she could look for the yellow envelope. Above her, the sky threatened grey again, the storm was returning.

Jane jumped out of her skin because of a loud knock on her windscreen. A tall, charming Romeo stood next to her car with the yellow plastic envelope in his hand. When Jane wound down the window, she did not recognise him at first. She blamed the weather...but what kind of woman cannot recognise her own imaginary husband?

'Well hello! I think this belongs to you!' the man handed her the parking ticket 'You look like a proper little damsel in distress to me!' he beguiled.

'Thank you' Jane Breathed. Yes, she had just thanked the hero for giving her a parking ticket and calling her a 'damsel'

'I'm Jane'

She did not quite catch his name because of the weather, but it sounded like he had said: 'I'm Gorgeous, can I take you for a cup of tea?'

The Reminder

Hope hardly dared to touch the lace and satin, it almost slipped out of her fingers. She was anxious because it belonged to someone else now. Lacking faith in herself, her hands shook as she meticulously packaged her wedding dress. Its ivory fragility, vulnerable and delicate. The sound of the packing tape, harsh against the cardboard, what if the bride who has bought it gets the fabric and lace caught up on the tape? Hope had been careful the previous year on her own wedding day. The day where the weather had smiled on Hope and Matthew, but less than one year later the wedding dress had been sold on the internet.

'That's the last of it, are you still alright to drop it at the post office on your way to work?'

'Yes, I said I would, anything for you!' Matthew picked up the box.

'At least it's going to a good home' Hope rolled her fingers over her wedding ring.

'Don't worry, you've still got me to remind you of the wedding, and we'll be on our feet in no time. We just need a few months to get straight. That's how it is these days, it's the cost of living' Matthew gave Hope a squeeze around her waist 'Let's go out this Saturday for a meal, we can stretch to that, can't we? The Rose and Crown are doing a meal deal if we get a table early'

'It's a date... let's get some ice cream on the way home, chocolate ice cream!' Hope sneaked in her favourite.

Saturday came, and the wedding dress would have arrived at its destination. Hope got ready for date night. Her wardrobe now depleted, the proceeds drained away on their debts.

'Are you ready Hope? Come on, we don't want to miss an early table!' Matthew called up the stairs.

'Ready!'

They arrived at the pub restaurant, it was fairly quiet for a Saturday, the new couple had plenty to say, catching up on the week's events. Then Matthew noticed that something was different about Hope, he even put his knife and fork down before he had finished eating, and that was saying something.

'Where's your wedding ring?!'

'Oh, I know! Sorry! I just couldn't put my hand on it when I was getting ready, I feel a bit weird not wearing it, to be honest, but we were in a rush weren't we?' Hope was talking rather fast and saying a lot of words. The truth was, the ring had not been in any of its usual places.

The following morning, the wedding ring was the first thing that Hope thought of. Her hand reached over to the bedside table, but it just was not there. She went into the bathroom, picked up the mirror, the toothbrush holder. She took everything off the little glass topped table next to the basin and put it back again. It just wasn't there. Matthew came up behind her in the bathroom, he put his arms around her and kissed the top of her head. He knew what his wife was worried about.

'Not here then? It'll turn up, I've never known you lose anything all the time we've been together' Matthew looked at Hope's eyes in the mirror and watched them glaze over with tears.

'I know! I never lose anything! I thought you would be the first one to lose your wedding ring! Not me! How many times have I rescued your car keys? I've never lost anything, I know where everything is, all the time'

'We'll find it, don't worry let's have some breakfast and then we'll look together' Matthew hugged Hope and she stopped crying. She had sold the wedding dress if she had lost her ring too, then she had nothing left of the day. Matthew made her a cup of tea and some toast and brought them to bed as though Hope was unwell.

'Right, let's try and re-trace your steps, that's what I always do when I've lost something. Can you remember taking it off yesterday?' Matthew used his serious voice.

Hope was crying and laughing at the same time.

'You don't retrace your steps! You just ask me if you've lost anything!' Hope sniffed

'Oh, it's a bit early for tears, trust me, it'll turn up,' Matthew said.

He came up with a plan for looking for the wedding ring. Hope had looked herself, and then Matthew went through the house lifting furniture, whilst Hope shone a torch underneath, blushing at the sight of dust in the corners, and remembered what her mother used to say about being 'thorough' but Hope worked and could not spend her life dusting. Hope sat down, deflated as her wedding dress had looked, wrapped up in the dry cleaner's plastic. She could hear Matthew opening and close every drawer in the bedroom. Yes, they had argued about Matthew's clumsiness. How he had accidentally put his work T-shirt and his smelly socks on a pile of fresh towels that Hope had folded. They had argued about him not emptying the dishwasher, and not hanging the clothes up to dry as she would have done. They should not be arguing so early into their marriage. She hoped that selling her wedding dress had not brought them bad luck. Matthew went outside and searched through the bins. He even put his hand down the toilet, such was his need to please his wife. He came over to where Hope was sitting and put his hand on the chair arm, she looked at his wrist. A strange reason to fall in love, but Matthew's wrist was one of the things she noticed when they first met.

'Well, I've not been able to find it yet, Hope, but trust me, sometimes things just turn up!' Hope disappeared into a pair of cupped hands, and then the tears started. She cried and cried, experiencing every stage of grief. Worst of all was the worry that the loss meant something. Was it a bad omen? Would she lose Matthew as well? She hoped not, he had such lovely wrists. Then she denied it, maybe Matthew was right, the ring would turn up somewhere in the house. Hope felt ashamed, losing a wedding ring was the type of disaster that no one wanted to admit to. How could she be so careless? Eventually, she cried herself to sleep.

The following morning, there was the usual rush getting ready for work, tripping up over one another, burning the toast.

'I'm going to work now. I'm not worried about the wedding ring, I have faith in you and me, that's what's important'

Hope went back upstairs to finish getting ready for work. She looked at her bedside cabinet, and sitting there as clear as day, appearing quite innocently and where it honestly had not been when they had looked one hundred times the day before... With no explanation, was Hope's wedding ring!... Matthew reminded Hope to trust him, and he had been right...

Swimmingly

I've been looking forward to today all week, I'm all prepared for dynamic, stabilising water movements on a certain afternoon. I've packed my exercise kit, my lucky towel, my plastic hairbrush. Everything I need is ready in advance. This special routine gets my mind focused in the zone, the aquatic competition mood. Soon after I arrive, I'm ushered into the changing rooms. I put on my swimming costume, whilst sitting on a bench it's a bit of a stretchy struggle, maybe it has shrunk in the wash? I'm feeling ambitious, and I imagine to myself that we had filmed ourselves dancing and singing. Making a video just like the Olympic diving team, had, filming themselves to celebrate the start of the games. They posted their film on the internet and it even made the headlines. Mixed synchronised swimming is a big bit of news, I'm sure we are going to be famous.

 'Hello everyone, are we all alright?' I say as I make my way into the pool area.

We all lineup, limber up one by one wearing matching bright elastic swimming caps. The warm water is caressing our bodies The blue reflective waves test our balance, challenging our senses. The sound of it, the familiar smell of swimming pools Side by side, gracefully making our way around the edge like dainty painted crabs, carefully closer to the middle, whilst our star performer is lifted into the centre, propelled quite high into the air for a dramatic entrance, the pride of our routine.

We manipulate our bodies, manoeuvring complicated movements, precisely, in time with the music. Showing off our aerobic, athletic strength and skill. Around in a circle one way, and then back again in another, making pretty patterns in the water. Legs and arms, our limbs show off our water ballet style, our determined endurance. On the tips of our toes and gracefully back down again, squatting, flying. One leg standing still and straight, the bottom leg pulled up to our chests like flamingos. The crowd cheers. The judges are near. Normally, in practice, there is time for gossip. Ann always has news for Greta about her children, Marion has a new puppy, and the things she does are so funny! Sue seems to have a new swimming costume every week. And Colin always has a joke to tell, we have a way of understanding each other against the noise of the swimming pool. We swim, we glide away from the side with skilful sets of symmetry. We anticipate high scores and give ourselves a well-deserved pat on the back. Life is not a competition, but we all set our own goals, we are only competing against ourselves. Striving to be the best. Well, can you tell me one good reason why not?

Really, we are not Olympians or part of any competitive sporting event. We are a group of people brought together by different sorts of disability, so in that way, we are part of a team; a club we never really wanted to join, but working together with our conditions in common, making the best out of what life has thrown at us. Hydrotherapy makes us stronger, no participation equals no recovery. 'Use it, don't lose it' the physiotherapist often says with encouragement.

Battling against a world where people are often assessed on looks, the imagined judges were not evaluating us, they were the carers, and the volunteers nearby to support us. And the crowds I saw at the side of the pool were the peculiar patterns painted on the tiles. If I squint my eyes they look like a crowd, three deep cheering us on. The elastic swimming caps were just an idea from Greta, she's originally from Germany and they are all the rage over there. Another session over, another therapy ticked off my weekly schedule, it's a full-time job keeping myself well. Exhausted from the effort, but exhilarated, energised in general.

'Will you be joining us next week?' Mary, the organiser of the programme asked.

'All being well' I say.

'How did your session go today?'

'Oh, just swimmingly' I answered.

Night Time Wonderings

My husband is a quiet man until he falls asleep. The night chorus that groans from the upper half of his body keeps me awake regularly. Tonight, he has turned over, taking the covers with him, whipping me out of the envelope I had cocooned myself into. There is no way I'm getting back to sleep now. I venture to the bathroom, and daringly switch on the light... 3.30am, the perfect time of night to admire myself in the full-length mirror, assess the shape am I in these days. Wearing my T-shirt and knickers. I return to bed, my mind still wandering... I'm not the only thing out of shape, these knickers are getting rather baggy! I looked at my phone, it was 3.45am, a quick glance at the internet. Social media is around us all the time these days. A woman I haven't seen since school has posted a comment about herself:
'Disgusted to find I was wearing knickers that did not match my bra! I've let myself go!'
Oh! Who cares? I'm bored now, mobile off! Eyes shut! It's no good...

So, everyone is thinking about underwear, not just me. Hang on a minute! The pair I'm wearing were bought as a pack of two! The other pair were cerise pink with tiny white spots, and I haven't worn them for quite some time. I remember when I bought them, oh that was four years ago, they probably got worn out and I threw them away. No, I'd remember; I'm funny about things like that. I wonder where could those knickers have got to? People always talk about missing socks like it's an actual phenomenon. That socks somehow get lost down the waste pipes of washing machines, clogging them up, reducing their efficiency. I could cringe! The thought of my pink spotty knickers clinging to the pipes...

This is stupid. I should get out of bed, turn the light on, look in the drawer, and find the missing underwear.. Second thought I'd better not, I'm guessing it's 5.30 AM by now, we'll be getting up for work soon. I'll look tomorrow. But what if I forget? It's a well-known fact that people forget what they have been wondering about during the night.

Now, which holidays have I taken those knickers on? The in-laws holiday cottage! Self-catering, washing machine included the real 'cottage experience'. A place for us to stay when we visit. A coastal cottage rented out in the summer. No break from laundry duty, so it is possible that those knickers had been abandoned in the cottage. The next people who stayed there might have found them. Or worse still, they could have joined their load of washing in the drum, and spun round with their towels and t-shirts! My unidentified pair of dark pinks ruining someone else's holiday, dying all their clothes a funny colour. Oh! I can imagine the wife holding my pink knickers up towards her husband's face, demanding 'Whose are these?!' They would argue. And then present them to my in-laws at the end of the week. My knickers would then be put in one of those polyethene sandwich bags, and returned to me at the next family gathering... 'I think you left these at our cottage!'

This was stupid if that had really happened it would have been resolved months ago. Why do I let my mind wander this way when I am trying to get back to sleep? Peace, relaxation, and sleep... sleep! Oh, I cannot wait for our next holiday...

Just as I was about to drift off, another thought struck me. I got out of bed for the second time and crept back along the landing. Moonlight was shining through the bathroom window, into my daughter's open bedroom door. My eyes were drawn to a pile of teenage clothes on the floor. I stepped forward, avoiding that creaky floorboard, my fingers pulled a pink triangle out of the pile. 'Yes! My knickers! Must have got mixed in the laundry! Thank goodness they are not still at the cottage!'

Night time wonderings ended, I finally fell back to sleep and dreamt of holidays.

Qu'est-ce que c'est

Genevieve Dubois was happiest when she was living in France. The language, the patisseries, the nonchalance. Her journey since those days involved countless tales of moving house, changing jobs, an inability to settle anywhere. Her most recent move was into the wet streets of Whitefield in North Manchester. Her adoptive son, Matteo's journey had started with an uncertain origin, somewhere in France. Followed by a tumultuous adventure of different schools, different friends, and now different jobs. Still living at home with his mother at age thirty, both of them getting to know different sets of new neighbours, now having opposing opinions of the current one's next door. The youngest daughter of the neighbours had been the first to introduce herself to the habitué duo. Gazing upon Matteo with wide adoration:

'You don't look like a Pisces...' she had gushed, but her efforts were rebuffed. Matteo had opted to keep his distance, but his mother, Genevieve had uncharacteristically acquainted herself. First, she had befriended the mother, Emma, bonding over the partaking of day-time cake eating. Then, it was Edna the eldest daughter who had enamoured herself to Mme Dubois. Disclosing one day that she was trying to learn a little French. Although Genevieve Dubois did not agree to teach Edna immediately, Edna had felt strangely drawn to Madame Dubois, and she to her.

Every time Genevieve sat in the front parlour next door, she would squint her eyes at the vase of red paper poppies, the vaguest reminder of France. There was no patisserie, no tricolour, no panache in 1970s Whitefield, and Genevieve Dubois stuck out like an exotic bird.

The nineteen seventies had been kind to Edna's appearance so far. Ponderous plastic sunglasses, intending to be glamorous, in a variety of colours, usually black. Flowered full-length garments of Polyester, usually black. Sometimes see through, but not on purpose. 1976 was the hottest summer on record.

Edging towards age forty, Edna had achieved little with her time, and time was ticking on. A failed artist, who, nevertheless, still called herself an artist. She had attended Art college when she was younger, had this made her a qualified artist? No one was asking ... Did anyone want to buy her paintings?... No one was asking. And yet Edna's occupation was that of 'artist', because, in between meals, Edna created paintings. Having a relaxed attitude towards money, she rebelled against the polite formality of society. Afforded, because of her parent's means and money. Without her father's money, there would be no nude self-portraits.

Without her neighbour, Genevieve she would not have had the encouragement to 'get out' and join a painting group.

'Better to paint a model, than your own reflection, mon- amie ' Genevieve had said in alluring Frenglish.

So Edna concurred, caftan and canvas flapping around her thighs... during the hottest summer on record.

Edna joined a painting group, not a class. They met in a Methodist Church hall, of all places. They specialised in capturing the female form. Students from Manchester University were paid to model for life drawing. Edna's paintings started to celebrate naked women, rather than a tracing of the third trimester of pregnancy.

It could have been local boys climbing trees, peeping through the church windows. It could have been members of the group bragging about their painting group at a fondue party. But eventually, word got out about the life drawing in the local area. Narrow-minded people were disgusted. There was a meeting amongst the church committee to decide if the painters were acting immorally. Fortunately, it was the nineteen seventies. The church minister was a vegetarian. It was decided that, as no students had been harmed during the paintings, the group could continue. The man who started the group was called Maurice. He was a fascination of colour, purple flares, mustard hair, and a turquoise tank top with nothing underneath (it was the hottest summer on record after all) Maurice minced up and down in the hall. Giving advice on how one should compose one's painting. And occasionally making dramatic black marks on his canvas. He was not a teacher or anything, he called himself an artist. A retired gentleman, who, because of previous conventions, gifted the group its easels.

Edna did not need any advice, thank you, but relished in the joy of meeting like minded people. People who liked painting people. She had formed a friendship with a lady, a retired housewife, Marie-Antoinette. Marie for short... Marie who had promised herself that she would nosy into Edna's life at today's group...

'Looks like it's going to rain, Edna,' her sister said 'It needs to rain, to wash all this heat away'

'See you when I get back Edith, I imagine you will be right there, behind the door, watching for when this rain of yours starts!' Edna rolled her eyes at her younger sister.

Edith's observation was right, the heat was unbearable, but clouds were gathering and greying the distant sky. Edna walked to the group. Past the shops, past the general post office, past the asylum. Today's model was called Sally. Life drawing did not take long. The hall was hired for two hours every Wednesday afternoon. The majority of those two hours were filled with Maurice enjoying the sound of his own voice. Time spent on mutual appreciation. Marie-Antoinette arrived late, she bustled in and sat next to Edna. She had some tale about her husband making her late, nodding at today's model.

'I think he wanted to catch a glimpse of you love!' Marie always looked like she was chuckling, shoulders moving up and down, cheeks glowing. She winked at Maurice. Turning to Edna, with a nudge of elbows 'What does your husband think of you coming here every week to ogle nudes?'

Being socially inept as Edna was, she did not take this as a rhetorical question. She started giving too much information...

'I don't have a husband... I've never been married, I live with my mother and sister' ... then she heard herself say 'Harold' and before she knew it, Marie-Antoinette had put down her paint brush, and was giving Edna her full attention (albeit still giggling) Edna was still talking, showering Marie with tales of woe, heartbreak, and Harold, from days long ago.

'So, you see, I was put off men after him!' All the while, Edna continued with her charcoal masterpiece. The shading in, the blending ... Maurice had cocked his left eyebrow in the charcoal's direction. Edna had the power of passion behind her creativity. And then Marie-Antoinette said:

'Aww, shame that for you love, I think you must have let him knock your confidence'

There it was, Harold getting the better of Edna, after all, those years. Edna angrily finished today's masterpiece, punishing her canvas, as though she was venting some hidden frustration... Edna drained all her energies with the charcoal lines, she stood back and sighed, admiring her own efforts. This was the best piece of art the group had ever seen. There was even talk of a permanent move to charcoal, but this did not sit well with their 'painting' name. Maurice was secretly jealous of Edna that day. Meanwhile, her mind still on the Harold story.

Wanting to change the subject, Edna enquired as to the origin of Marie-Antoinette's name 'Are you French?'

'OH no,' more chuckling 'My father just liked how it sounds in a Mancunian accent'

The two women walked out of the church hall

'Only your name sounds French, and our neighbours are French... I thought you might know them?' Edna was trying to look sophisticated, there was nothing more sophisticated to Edna than having a French neighbour. Marie- Antoinette nodded and giggled.

'Are you having a lift home love? 'im indoors'll be here in a minute in the Cortina'

'Oh, no thank you, I'd rather walk' Edna rebuffed the offer, on account of her new friend getting her Harold story wrong. It must have been the way she told it.

'OK, love, if you're sure, only it looks like it's going to rain...'

The sky was no longer a skimpy summer dress sky.

'See you next week love' Marie-Antoinette got in her husband's Ford Cortina, and they sped off. Sure enough, the heavens opened as Edna was walking home. Her polyester caftan was wet through before she had even got past the asylum. By the time she turned on to her Avenue, the drawing of Sally's naked body had been completely rained off the canvas. Nipples and all.

Edna's sophisticated French neighbour was stood smoking at her front door.

'I 'ave just seen your mother and sister going to the market,' she said, extinguishing her cigarette in the tiny metal grill. Edna had forgotten her key, Mme Dubois invited her in. Edna followed Mme Dubois up the stairs. Edna started talking and explained the whole sorry story about her best piece of art, and about the Harold story being misunderstood. By the time they had got to the second floor, Genevieve Dubois knew all about the ruined artwork, and all about Harold.

Mme Dubois put her head on one side and took Edna in 'Tell me more about this 'arold person' she said his name as though she was sucking a lemon. Edna delighted in telling her, amongst other things...

'Well. He was really condescending... Even though he was the loser! Not me! I'm not a loser!'

'So, initially, he was dishonest about what kind of relationship he wanted. Then he was self-absorbed, parading you in front of another woman he still desired?' She clicked her tongue against the roof of her mouth in a sharp tut 'He was not man enough for you, Edna. What did you expect from an imbecile like that?' Madame Dubois put things so succinctly, yet without Edna realising, she had meant that Edna 'only had herself to blame'.

'Yes! Yes! Genevieve! That's exactly it !' Edna felt she knew Mme Dubois well enough to address her by her first name 'All these years I have been trying to explain how Harold put me off men for life!' Edna looked around Genevieve's front room. Dove grey blinds. Turquoise, silk screened wallpaper with a Chinoiserie bird pattern. A white Damask couch that was shaped in such a way, squint your eyes and it could be a chaise longue.

'Your front room is lovely!' said Edna. Genevieve put two coffees on the glass-topped coffee table. She looked at Edna, the overweight failure wearing clothes that did not suit her.

'Matteo is at work, I 'ave an idea' she was perched on the edge of her couch 'Why don't I let you draw me? It will make up for the afternoon disaster, the rain?'

'Yes it would, Genevieve, but I am a little embarrassed' Edna felt different around Genevieve, there was nothing more sophisticated than a French neighbour, after all.

Where Edna *imagined* herself as sophisticated, Genevieve had no need to imagine. She was still looking at Edna.

'Is it because I will be naked?' Genevieve raised her eyebrows and tipped her head to one side 'It is an English thing, you are shy to get undressed in front of one another! You English! If I ask you 'ca-va?' you all say 'fine I'm fine thank you!' Everybody is fine! Like your mother, even when her husband died she was 'fine!' ... If you were to ask me how I am I could probably give you a long list of 'ca ne vas pas'....'

Genevieve was speaking very quickly and Edna did not understand some of it. She had been sitting on the Damask furniture, mustering up some confidence. It may have been the mention of her Father that did it. Mme Dubois had been right. Mother did not sleep for weeks after Father died, but she was 'Fine, thank you'

Edna dusted down her canvas, it was not completely blank but the previous charcoal had given it a nice grey wash for the background. She reached into her crocheted rope bag and got out her charcoals. Sitting up straight, with some of her old confidence Edna declared

'I think you will make a very attractive model, Madame!'

'Merci!' Genevieve said

Mme Dubois perched on the end of one of her chairs, naked. It was a hot June day. The rain had stopped and the sun was shining through the blinds.

Edna asked Mme Dubois about living in France, why she had moved to England and how she had come to adopt Matteo. Edna really wanted to ask Genevieve how old she was. She looked fantastic for her age... whatever that might be. She looks amazing, Edna thought.

Genevieve gave away her nakedness, and some of herself on that day. It was a story that she had stuck to over the years. Told so many times it became true. She spoke very quickly about France, Matteo's orphanage, her relative in the south of England. The tale was interjected with plenty of 'Oui,' and 'Oui?' Genevieve spoke freely of all the jobs and various places they had lived in over the years. She spoke and spoke, but at the end, Edna knew very little about Genevieve Dubois, there had been no mention of a 'Monsieur Dubois' no mention of a French family, or why Madame Dubois had a French phrase book on her shelf.

Mme Dubois had left France and had been in England ever since.

Edna had squared up the portrait and had started drawing out Genevieve's frame on the canvas. Madame Genevieve Dubois had weaved herself a fancy life and even she could not keep up sometimes.

There was shading and blending in happening on Edna's side of the canvas. Edna tried to impress Genevieve by closing one eye and moving her thumb vertically and horizontally. Edna had seen other artists do this, she had no idea however that she was judging perspective.

Genevieve continued her story, there were many tales of Matteo not being able to settle, they tried the Midlands, South Manchester... Until the final part of the story involving Matteo finally feeling at home in North Manchester.

Genevieve was trying to peep over the top of the picture. She wrapped a shawl around her shoulders.

Life drawing does not take long.

'Voila!' Edna said as she turned the canvas around. Maurice's promise that 'practice makes perfect' had materialised. She was pleased with herself, and with the likeness, she had captured of Mme Genevieve Dubois. Genevieve went into the other room and came back dressed in a full-length wrap-around of her own. Edna suspected this was her housecoat.

'Edna, d'accord?' Genevieve had a gold can of hairspray, which she used to set the charcoal drawing 'I think it's wonderful, magnifique, merci-beaucoup!'

Genevieve lightly perched herself next to Edna and did something unexpected. Mme Dubois held Edna's face with both hands and kissed her fully on the mouth. Edna's eyes widened. Genevieve's eyes were shut.

The two women looked at each other.

Genevieve glamorous, like a bottle of French perfume.

Edna ordinary, like a half used bottle of bubble bath.

Matteo, home from work, arriving at the top of the stairs just at that moment, like a scene from a classic French farce.

Tangling

Bending sliding, sliding bending, bending sliding. Repeat again, bend slide, and so on. The worm's light receptive cells reacted to the unnatural shine of the fermenting machine. 'Did you know? Contrary to popular belief, if a worm is chopped in half, it will not survive'. Wandy knew this instinctively because instinct is how worms get the idea about stuff. This worm's general knowledge was quite good, for a worm. Bending, sliding, as Wandy burrowed its head under the plastic wall, it increased its speed, by taking an extra long stride. With so many predators, birds, badgers and baby gardeners (helping Grandad's garden with risky plastic spades) Wandy instinctively knew it had to hide. The worm belonged to a species with such a wide lifespan (a few days to six years) ... It had lasted this long, it would be a shame... Life is too short to worry about the past. Too short actually for the short fat worm Wandy used to tangle with, slurped and snaffled into the hungry mouth of a passing badger like a spaghetti main. Wandy the worm was sliding away, and leaving it all behind.

The worm instinctively knew the fermenting machine was its desired destination. It was so dark. So moist. So hot. So right! Wandy burrowed its tiny bristles into the mulch and pulled itself forward. Deeper, buried, safer. Its senses were on fire. Rich, fermenting fire! Wandy's skin was alive with the exchange of putrid gases, it felt centimetres longer! Forward, curled, sleepy. Wandy had buried itself into a spherical ball, inside the remains of a discarded Victoria plum. It's amazing how long those stones can hold their shape for.

'Do you know? If us earthworms really sleep?' Wandy wondered it felt like sleep but was it sleep? A sleep without dreams? All sentient beings need to regenerate, switch off their senses and reimburse the day's energy supplies. Wandy, despite no sense of time, instinctively knew it had been in its dormant state for long enough, rested, time invested, with no purpose now than survival, in its new life, leaving it all behind.

Wandy spent a long time burrowed at the bottom of the compost bin. Familiar textures of the garden leaf. And new sensations of banana skins, apple cores, pineapple prickles... and tea bags. New variety, for this worm's extra long colon.

'Did you know, that with no 'eyesight' to speak of, burrowing earthworms can survive underground, especially within the confines of a fermenting machine?' Wandy's internal dialogue was intelligent 'Gardeners need not hunt worms to speed up their process, earthworms will happily seek habitat in this decaying environment'. Wandy knew this, instinctively, of course, that is how worms get the idea about stuff don't forget. Happily? That word needed careful consideration. The worm was safe and self-sufficient, it had slid away from past reminders of its previous tangle partner. It had no recollection of its egg's nesting positions, Wandy's children could be anywhere.

It was happy in the hope, that those baby worms had the sense to seek solace in the soil sanctuary. Wandy had everything it needed. Self-sufficiency swapped for its previous animal behaviours. Surfacing when rain vibrates the earth, for an hour (no more) of transportation to another place. Wandy did not need to travel now, but habit was tempting, even if the worm had lasted that long. Yes. Wandy belonged to a species with a seemingly unfair supply of enemies, it was not expecting what came next, however. Who would have credited it? Worm on worm violence! Wandy was unable to settle, feeling uncomfortable in the knowledge there were enemies within, it just instinctively knew. 'Did you know, that worms are hermaphrodites? I am neither boy or girl'. Proud was Wandy of this, but a partner was still required for worms to spread their genes 'That's what we're here for isn't it?'

Nature takes over, rain falls, beating its rhythm on the ground, the soil, the life-giving soil. Wandy, with no sense of time, spent long enough making its way to the surface. Bending sliding, bend slide, and so on tiny bristles pulling further. Coiling a path upwards towards the sky, the lid of the fermenting machine. Wandy had been expecting to come face to face with other worms, comrades, and counterparts, it could sense them, instinctively. But this worm had felt a sense of unease and was right to do so.

"Look at the size of it! Ha! Look at the size of its belt!"

Wandy tried to hide in amongst some leaves.

"No use in trying to hide! Look at the size of you, greedy worm have you been gorging our bounty on your way to the top?"

Wandy considered this question, before instinctively answering it. The decaying food had been all consuming, burrowing through had meant *eating* through, and of course, eating had meant depositing. That *is* what Wandy was supposed to be doing... There had been a deep orange coloured structure, it's side had felt cold and smooth until Wandy reached the roughly cut, moist edge. The worm had stuck its head inside, pungent gases exchanged, an unfamiliar smell of matches. Wandy had recoiled.

'I don't think it likes our pumpkin!' the skinny pink worm said to the even skinnier worm, with a bewitching black head.

"I was born inside a pumpkin, how dare you!" The bewitching worm thrashed her tail. Minuscule prickles whipped Wandy's flabby, pulsating flesh.

"I burrowed in here to hide... from death" Wandy defended.

'Hide from *death!*'

'Yes,' Wandy bowed its head. The two worms looked at one another, and then laughed a callous laugh. Who would have credited it? Mean girl pumpkin worms!

'Who is this *death* you speak of, Fatty?' Wandy lifted its head to answer, but not quickly enough for the spoilt worm.

'Speak! Don't instinct! I'm not a mind reader!'

Wandy opened its mouth, which was only designed for burrowing, forcing itself to form words it started to speak:

'Death is when the short fat worm I used to tangle with was suddenly taken away!'

The two spoilt worms instinctively formed their own mouths into a shocked 'O' shape.

'YOU? ... Have tangled?'

Their puny minds no longer interested in death, gossip presented itself for investigation.

'Yes,' Wandy hung its head with the shame of an off-white bride.

'Who? ... in the garden... would tangle with a night crawler like you!'

The pumpkin worms threw themselves into the bottom of the pumpkin's inside, laughing and coiling. Wandy sniffed around for an escape route, sliding up around the pumpkin's outer shell, too large for even Wandy to fit inside its mouth. It slid back down again, landing on the crisscross pattern of carrot peelings. Wandy heard whispering, and instinctively knew it was about itself. Wandy lifted its light receptors. Two snakes popped out of the pumpkin's left eye.

'Are you a girl worm, or a boy worm?' One of the pumpkin worms asked a stupid question.

'I'm just a worm' Wandy answered.

'Worms who's names begin with 'S' are women, and worms who's names begin with 'H' are men! I'm Sath, and this is Sote!'
Their names sounded sinful, their question confusing.
'My name is Wandy'
'Your name begins with 'W'?! Oh, this is priceless! You've given yourself a 'W' name! You don't look the precocious type! The only people who are allowed to name themselves beginning with 'W' are worms! You are doing it wrong! You haven't understood correctly!' Sath screamed, making little sense.
'Well, I am a worm! Not a *person* !' Wandy tried to crawl into the cracks of the carrot peel. Sath and Sote continued whispering and giggling.
'We've got an idea! Seeing as you've stolen our soil, you can provide us with a service. Suck up the soil, so you look even fatter, and we look even thinner' Sote said, it was the first time she had spoken. And Wandy had foolishly thought she was going to be kind! Not so, she was just as snide as Sath.
'Yes, you'll make us look good, sliding next to you, a big juicy fat worm!'
Wandy could have easily squashed these spoilt little worm-girls, but decided against it, instinctively knowing she was part of a plan.

'What's wrong Wandy? You don't have to look good, you've already tangled... I'm going to rename you 'Slag' !'

Wandy was affronted. The worm had no idea what a 'slag' was, but it did not sound good. Wandy was not a slag, nor a slug, and not stupid.

'Who, in the *garden* are you making yourself look good for?' It was a risk, but Wandy had to say something these stupid worms had made themselves sisters, unable to do what worms do best... *tangle...*

'For Grandad! Of course! We're making ourselves look good for Grandad!' Sath professed.

'Grandad?'

'Yes, he lifts the lid, and...'

'I like his plastic shovel the best, makes me feel like I'm living on the edge!' Sote interrupted Sath, she would pay for this later. 'The sunshine makes us burn, but we know it's worth it because of Grandad. Of the way he makes us *feel'* Sath coiled with romance. Sote slid her head next to her. If they were not so emaciated, their belts would be bulging.

'Careful girls, you don't want to tangle with each other!'

The two spoilt worms flung themselves apart, poked over the top of the pumpkin and spat at Wandy, but it was worth it.

'You want me to eat as much of these rotting vegetables as I can?'

'YES!' The spoilt worms chorused.

'Bring it on!' Wandy folded itself in two and took an extra long slide up the side of the pumpkin, mouth open wide, soon filled full of mulch from the chopping board, tea bags batted away.

'Bye, Slag!' Sath said 'Yeah, bye Slag!' The two mean worms coiled and wriggled, dancing a snake dance that only they thought was attractive.

Time continued inside the adopted confines of the fermenting machine. Wandy's instincts naturally returned to the sensation of safety. Most fools know that worms have a specific job to do as the underground saviours of mankind. For the next full moon, or so, Wandy minded her own business, recycling waste and producing soil. What goes in, must come out. Sath and Sote would leave her alone for so long, Wandy was left uninvited to their precious pumpkin. To be fair, that's how Wandy preferred it. Occasionally, they would opt to remind the worm of their presence. "Hey, Slag! Catch a teabag!"

They would throw a tattered teabag at Wandy (I bet you didn't know that worms could throw) They would tease, torment and tightly squeeze any remaining self-respect Wandy had. And she had quite good general knowledge for a worm do not let that be forgotten. Like bored housewives, Sath and Sote dismissed their rightful recycling occupations and promoted themselves to the management and murderous manipulation of Wandy- the worm that had once tangled. As mentioned previously, sometimes the abuse was direct: "Hey Slag" this and "Hey Slag" that. But mostly, the bullying was slippery, secretive and spiteful. Not only was Wandy never invited into the pumpkin, regular pumpkin parties would take place, for other members of the fermenting machine (beetles, centipedes and stray spiders) This always took place in full view of poor Wandy, who was never welcome. Still, the worm had to admit, survival would be worth it. Wandy had grown so long and lived so long, it would be a shame to say goodbye to life now. Sath and Sote's inescapable sarcasm started to prove stressful for Wandy. The worm tried to bring peace, even trying to suck up to the pumpkin worms, bringing foraged gifts from in and around the compost bin, seeds and so on. But the bullying continued, and became snide; were they saying things for Wandy's benefit? When usually they worked in pairs, sometimes Sath and Sote would split up, and pick away at Wandy's subconscious.

"You know that present you gave Sath?"

"Yes"

"Well, promise you won't say I said anything, but she didn't like them. Wrong seeds, you see. Silly Slag, better luck next time!" Sote sneered.

Then another time, Sath cornered Wandy to complain about her own inability to burrow in a straight line.

"I just can't slide straight, Slag, know what I mean?"

Straight lines had never occurred to Wandy. Zig-zagging happily- but Sath's words had stolen any remaining smiles. Wandy lay awake, sacrificing her dreamless sleep, thinking over Sath's words. Did she mean that for her? Was this survival? Or was this suicide?

With no sense of time, Wandy could not tell how long it had been, but for a species with so many enemies, it was not long before mild peril arrived at the compost bin.

The plastic lid flung open, revealing the sun. This lid never ever opened in the rain. Sath and Sote wriggled, flirted and coiled. In her excitement, Sote even expelled a little soil. And then Grandad spoke:

'Hello, my beauties, making me some compost for my borders?'

Wandy thought the two mean worms were going to faint with Grandad-mania. She had to admit that his voice had a rather soothing quality. Enjoyment of the human voice came all too soon, though, the worm had come to expect enemies and was all prepared.

'Grandad! Grandad! Look at my plastic spade' A softer, baby voice spoke. Wandy knew she must not be tempted by these sweet vibrations and slid off the pumpkin, into the safety of the leaves.

'You be careful, little one, now what's this?' Grandad looked down into his compost bin and frowned a furrowing frown.

'He's different today, what's wrong?'

'He usually swirls a big stick around!'

The two pumpkin worms squealed, their strong sense of entitlement easily squashed. Wandy was now on the inside plastic edge of the fermenting machine, safe in the knowledge this was where she was meant to be.

'I did tell your Grandma not to put your Halloween pumpkin in whole! It's too big for any worm to swallow! No wonder these two look a bit skinny!'

'What's he saying, Sote?' Sath said. But it was too late. Grandad lifted the pumpkin out of the compost bin and rested it on the wall.

'Heeeelp!' The pumpkin worms squealed, of course, they could not be heard.

'Grandad, Grandad! Do you want my plastic spade?' The baby gardener said.

'No, Jemima, I need to find some gardening tools to cut up your pumpkin, you help Grandad, and look after these worms'

'Oooooh!' enthused the baby gardener.

'Ahhhhh!' Screamed the worms

Wandy heard everything, it peeped through the little crack in the fermenting machine's plastic. Sights, lights, and gases, the worm could instinctively tell what was going to happen next. Wandy could hardly bear to be reminded of previous entanglements, but the little girl's fingers were just like short, fat worms. Jemima picked up Sote in between her thumb and forefinger, lifted her arm, cocked her head back and opened her mouth.

'Jemima! No! Don't eat the worms! Put it on the grass please, there's a good girl!'

'Put me back in the fermenting machine please, little girl!' Sote's silent worm voice meant nothing to Jemima.

'See, I told you I was Grandad's favourite!' Sath said, but it was too late, pecked and picked in a Blackbird's beak like hors d'oeuvres. Just like that, she was gone.

'Birdy! Birdy! Grandad! A bird just ate that worm!' Jemima giggled. Wandy watched on.

'Very good, stand back now, I've found something to smash the pumpkin with'
And just like that, it was gone.

'And I've got something to cut worms in two with!' Jemima said, and just like that, Sote was gone.

Grandad carefully threw the pumpkin pieces back into his compost bin. The movement of the decaying waste made Wandy bounce to the top.

'Well, look at the size of you! You're a beauty! Jemima! Look, look at this gigantic worm!'
Wandy froze on the surface of the bin.

'Put the lid back on Grandad, and then it can make some soil!'

'Right- o Jemima! What would we do without worms?'
And just like that, Wandy was happy.

The Mystery of Sight

Reality TV has exploded into a competitive market. All celebrities that could possibly be bought with a cheeky nought on the end have been explored and exploited. Over the years, careers have been re-launched and re-hashed, only to be ruined by the tabloid press, failed engagements and publishing of previous promiscuity.

And don't even get me started on the non-celebrity reality TV. There appear to be hundreds of reality programmes covering a wide range of subjects. Making stupid people famous. Society has been drained to the very dregs of its talent, although younger generations have become wise to it, opting to promote themselves in self-styled internet video clips. Yes, I know that's how it started for me, the all-American series of horrible housewives exported to the UK ... those were the days. I got my teeth fixed for free, and made myself a millionaire fake lifestyle with fake friends. I was the best one! Got my own spin-off show! Those days still haunt me. Apparently, there is still a twitter account dedicated to my meltdown.

The producers set me up. Watching housewives is pretty boring, without the scripted bit, that is. I was meant to be having the wedding of all weddings. It was meant to be the series finale, but instead of '*Next time on the reality housewives of Manchester*' scenes of my nuptials, they screened '*Today, on a very special episode of RHOM*' The trailer showed me screaming, black mascara streaming down my face, when the penny dropped and I realised the scene I had walked in on. I could have been a footballer's wife if it was not for those producers. What I hadn't known couldn't harm me, I would have been rich. Now look at me, look at that twitter account! I cannot even bring myself to think about it. Even though I am a pretty crier.

I've moved on. Requests for public appearances dried up, magazines no longer want me for photo shoots. I launched my own waterproof mascara range, which I thought was a stroke of marketing genius, but no one bought it. I've been bankrupt twice, whilst my ex-fake friend is living my luxury life in my luxury mansion. I don't even want to think about it. Just as I was about to make it into the gossip pages of the tabloids once again (because I had signed on benefits) I got an offer.

The celebrity booking agency that I used to be connected with had re-named and re-branded themselves as 'Reel Real' (which is meant to be a play on words). They got in touch.

'Hun! Hun, it's me, Rashida! Have you missed me, hun? How do you fancy being famous again?'

Again?! Her Yorkshire accent from London took me right back there on my answer machine. Famous again! I cannot go anywhere without someone mentioning... something, or giving me a double take like I'm a long-lost school friend they nearly recognised. I'm *still* famous. Anyway, I was soon on all expenses paid economy class trip down to London, drinking chai tea and eating Rashida's bulldust about an approach from Little Mouse documentary makers.

'It's not really reality TV as such, well depends on what you believe in...' Rashida said, she doesn't look a day older than when she was my agent in the housewife days. She still spits a little spit when she says words like 'such' though.

'What do you mean? What I believe in?' I asked. Rashida smirked a little smile, latte glistened on her top lip.

'Do you believe in ghosts?'

....

What a waste of time!

Well, I'm back on the train going home, up north again, all that way. I keep my shades on, prescription sunglasses, that way no one will know I wear spectacles and no one will recognise me either.

'Don't I know you from somewhere?' The Virgin Rail ticket collector interrupted my train of thought. I opened my mouth to speak, but it turns out he is mistaken.

Back to my e-reader, it lights up, I can read it, I can see perfectly with these glasses on like I've got perfect sight. Can't beat a bit of 'chick lit', I stumbled on this author in the free book section, her stories are full of swear words, spelling and storyline errors but she certainly knows how to hook the reader! Sex and stereotypes? Yes, please! For ordinary people, a champagne lifestyle is the type of thing that you can only read about, but this author has done her research! These characters are so believable! Believable to the likes of me anyway... A character's whirlwind romance, feet sweeping, heartbreaking, revenge seeking, protagonist comes-up-smelling-of-roses-three hundred pages later, and I'm back in Manchester. Ahh, Manchester Piccadilly. The big glass panel, the escalators to the expanding Metrolink system spreading silver tram tracks like spider's webs all over the city. There was a girl wearing a high visibility jacket handing out free copies of the Manchester Evening News. That's when I saw it.

....

'Rashida! Rashida! Ring me back, as soon as you get this! Sign me up! I'll do anything! Jungle, dancing, cooking! Any variety of celebrity realism you like!'

I had treated myself to a black cab home, the driver had started to reveal himself to be chatty.

'Aren't you the...'

'Yes, yes... Just drive me home!' I said, he had the same copy of today's local news on his front seat.

'I reckon you could sue, love, £17.20 on the meter...' He said as he pulled into my driveway.

'Keep the change' I said throwing him a twenty-pound note. My boots walking up my modest gravel path comforted me, I was bursting for the loo. Did not even notice the cello taped notice on my front door. My key doesn't work!

A few minutes later, the penny dropped, and so did my drawers, unfortunately. I had no choice, I was bursting! Next door's security light was swiftly followed by their cat, observing me squatting amongst the ornamental topiary. I read the eviction notice, and wondered if there was celebrity version of *'Can't pay? We'll take it away!'* That I could have appeared in.

'I told them!' My neighbour appeared instead. 'I said! I told them you'll be back in a bit, that you don't go out much! I warned them! I warned them you might have a breakdown! I showed them the YouTube clip!'

Weighing up the situation, with only the eviction notice, the Manchester Evening News and a designer handbag to my name, I decided to accept my horrific neighbour's invitation to go inside her house for a cup of tea.

'Oh, it says here that you *still haunt them, to this day!* Well, they got that wrong, how can you haunt them if you don't get out often? I would sue if I was you!'

The article in the newspaper was not even about me. It was about my two ex's, my ex-footballer, and my ex-friend. They have just had yet another baby, refurbished *my* house again, but the main bit of news was her charity work.

Must be a slow news day in Manchester. I had skim read the article in the taxi and eventually found my name. The paragraph had started with:

'*Of course, it hasn't always been plain sailing for...*'

They are claiming that I still try and 'haunt' them, that I am still trying to be in their lives. Alright, so I did try and claim my credit card bills were his. Who wouldn't? He had paid out for the wedding, and that had included the rings that I kept and sold and designer shoes, plus emergency shoes. After what happened, I went on another spending spree... a couple of (twenty-or-so) times to get over the mental torment I was caused. It was his fault. And yes I have written things on social media directed at them, but that's not my fault! I think about what they did to me every single day...

'Are you ok, love? Only I've got to start making our evening meal...'

My neighbour has not stopped talking since I started re-reading the newspaper. Now I think she wants me to leave.

Emergency overnight kit and check in at Manchester's Premier Inn executed, Rashida finally gets back to me, they must work long hours in the talent agency business.

'No, sorry love, the prime-time shows want celebs that have at least got their own Wikipedia page. It's for launch night so that viewers can 'Google' the contestants. What's that? Celebrity evictions? No, it's really this ghost show they want you for, listen to this title, though, love, '*The Mystery of Sight'* that's what it'll be called, snappy isn't it?'

'I'll take it' I said.

And just like that, the following day, I was on all expenses paid economy class journey to the north east. The closer you get to Scotland, haunted castles pop up like clichés in a horror movie. Trains, coaches, and a driver. Anyone would think Britain was a big island.

'Here she is! Here's our star!' The man who is recognisably the director threw his arms out wide, but then turned his head to the side, out of my earshot 'We're not using 'Real Reel' again, I wanted Biggins for this!' He turned back to me, and my fur headband that forgives anyone's bad hair day. 'Hello, darling, let's get you in hair and wardrobe... and makeup, filming starts as soon as the sun goes down. You've met Maggie haven't you?' He flips his hand in the air. Maggie? There was just an elderly lady under a lace shawl reading a tablet, the light flickering on her face, which at that angle is not a good look. Soon, I'm ushered, fed, watered and dressed inside a portable trailer. Maggie turns out to be the medium they are using to summon the ghosts, although, at first glance, I thought I had recognised her from 1970s children's television.

'Tonight. On *The Mystery of Sight,* we'll be investigating the unknown ghost. The ghost that is brave enough to be heard, but is refusing to be *SEEN*!'

I sound quite good, don't I? Maggie is right behind me, still with the black lace shawl covering her head, but now has a torch shining up on her face from below. There have been reports at the castle of visitors getting poked in the back, singing, banging and screaming heard from other rooms. All these goings on have manifested in some way that cannot be seen. Not like the other ghosts of this castle, they've all been seen. Seen, recorded and advertised on the tourist website. This is not the first camera crew that has visited, and we won't be the last. Take after take well into the night, with the promise of sensational, dramatic effects being added later. We have paranormal paraphernalia, night vision contraptions. Maggie the medium keeps gasping and grabbing my arm, annoying, but the director says it creates suspense. My shocked face is going to be the cliff-hanger before the commercial break.

'Great 'shocked face' darling, I knew you would have a good 'shocked face' when I saw what an ugly crier you are!' The director said... and I thought I was a pretty crier, not my fault I've had to cut back on Botox. I hope he has a good supply of dramatic effects because even my face can't turn this schedule filler into a rating winner. By the way, my shocked face was due to the noise that the lighting man was making getting his equipment inside, single handed. Compared to '*Reality Housewives'* this is a tiny crew, although admittedly a stylist budget is not required. I am so tired now, train journeys, eviction from my (comparatively modest) home... my return to work. This time last week, if you'd have told me, that I would be sat in a freezing castle singing for my supper, I would have spat my Prosecco out. How many hours have we been at it? Still no ghost. 'When are we going to solve the *Mystery of Sight*?' I breathe into the camera.

'And cut! Let's take a break, people!' The director claps his hands. The camera man looks like he's going to have a coronary.

'When are we going to get off? And how are we getting to the hotel?' I close the door of the trailer and turn to Maggie. Then I'm doing my shocked face again. Turns out the lace shawl is attached to a wig. Maggie is messing about with her eyes and removing these weird grey contact lenses.

'I'm itching like buggery under here!' Maggie the medium's haunting necromancy is replaced by a warm Scouse accent 'There's no hotel love, and we've done when we've done!'

'Oh, you're joking!' I turn to Maggie, she is now re-doing her 'wrinkles' 'Pass me that pan stick, will you doll, they hired someone local to do our make-up before, but she's long gone now'

This is all very strange, I spend time and money getting my wrinkles blasted out of my face with Botox, this woman is enhancing hers with an eyebrow pencil.

'How long have you been a medium then?'

'Ha!' she nearly drops her cigarette 'I used to be a medium, but I'm a large now!' She looks at me and her face changes when she realises 'Oh, you're not joking, are you? I'm an actress, same as you! Well, not same as you, you're a whatcha meh call it?' She is waving a makeup brush in my direction 'A reality celebrity? I'm just an actress, have to be signed up to a union, different rates doll'

'A union?'

'Yes, that's why there are more reality celebrities than actors... You are cheaper..'

'Cheaper!' My shocked face is working overtime, same as me.

'Which agency are you with?'

'Real Reel' I say.

'Never heard of 'em! Are they new?'

'Yes, it's the same agent that, well the same woman.. anyway, they offered me a flat rate for the whole series'

'Well! You're here till the death then, same as me! No shame in it, love, I have to take what I can get these days'

Then there was a tinny sounding banging on the trailer door.

'Come on girls, round three!' One of the crew said.

We walked around the creaky corridors, up the spiral staircase, into each dusty room, clinging on to any creak, sound or shuffle we may or may not have heard.

I am struggling to read my scripted bit with my prescription sunglasses, so I have to ad-lib.

'Are we the only people in this hall? Please give us a sign'

'A sign is alllll we neeed' Maggie echoed behind me.

'Did you hear that?' I repeat several times. This gives the producer the chance to edit in a load of re-plays of ghost action.

'Sounds like a chair scraping across the floor' That sort of thing. I also had to read out bits and pieces about why a ghost would possibly want to hang around here. There is a servant, who used to look after the treasures. A little girl with a balloon, no explanation but apparently little girl ghosts are thought to be the scariest. These have been apparitions, but the ghost we are after is a mystery because no one has actually seen it, only heard it, or been touched by it. Patrons of the castle are getting worried because the ghost is actually scaring people off the ghost tours. They haven't been able to renew their business insurance after the ghost made some bloke have a heart attack. Apparently, at first he said that it was 'one of those things' he is on cardiac medication, but is a big fan of travelling around, going on all the ghost tours, he even said 'It's my own fault, for scaring myself to death' ... Well, he soon changed his tune apparently, when the accident litigators got hold of him. So here we are, it's a win-win situation. The castle gets paid for us making the 'documentary' and the public get to see the dangerous ghost banished.

We carry on, around the risk assessment free building. Then the camera man's face changes, he goes white and starts peeping over my shoulder. I carry on talking into the camera until I hear a loud thump.

....

If you'd have told me a week ago that I would have been stuck on my own in the middle of nowhere, with no phone signal, trying to revive a reality TV cameraman, I would have spat my Prosecco out. At least I managed to solve the 'mystery' of sight, but unfortunately, it was only partly caught on camera. The ghost, that if seen causes the recipient of said vision to have a heart attack. Happens every time, it's not really the ghost's fault. It wasn't my fault either, and that's why I had to take 'Real Reel' to court after they initially refused to pay me my flat rate for the entire series of *The Mystery of Sight*. We had our day in court, but it was a done deal. You see, Rashida and myself came to an arrangement, it was, of course, the celebrity version of *Courtroom Drama* the daytime no-nonsense litigation show, that we appeared on.
'How do you think I did, hun?'
'Oh, you're a natural!' I said.

'Right, well don't spit your prosecco out, but I've had an offer come in for you. Such a good offer' Rashida was back in business.
'What is it?' I was expecting Thursday evening prime time on one of the four *at least*.
'*Celebrity Benefits City*' Rashida had latte on her top lip 'What's the matter? You're not the only reality star on benefits!' Rashida's maroon fingernail slid a upturned piece of paper over to me 'Look at the flat rate they're offering, you'll soon see it's not such a mystery why celebrities agree to do these programmes!'
Rashida was right, and her business was booming: 'Reel Real talent agency, where the celebrities *really* will do anything'

Madame Cézanne

'What is wrong, my love?'

'I had the strangest night's sleep. A dream, I dreamt something so strange, my dear, so vivid'

'Vivid?'

'Oui, oh, it was nothing' I say, as chalk dust billows around his face, illuminated by the sun shining through our window pane. I capture this image, to save in my memory 'I will see you later'

'A bien tot, Môn Amie'

Rose bushes accessorise every doorway I pass, more noticeable to me in the Paris sunshine. Here I am, at work, I sigh. My day is to be a dusty one, protecting prose from mischievous bookworms. Today felt repetitive, folding, glueing, stamping, binding. I found myself drifting, imagining, wishing. That dream was so vivid, my mind returned to it several times during the day, I could not get those images of out of my head. There had been something very distant and unworldly about the women in my dream, and that is what had unsettled me.

Later that same day, in the evening, my artist lover and *moi* shared a bottle of French wine and mused over his latest piece of watercolour.

'I think I will title this one 'Madame Cézanne with Hortensia' he reached for my hand as he spoke.

'But you have not made me *Madame'* I teased, I withdrew my hand, and hid my sweet face behind a piece of bread.

'One day, my darling!' Cezanne said.

He has been here eleven years longer than I, what is he waiting for? What is he frightened of? His parents? Marriage? Women themselves? I looked at my lover's painting, my own face with perfect skin hiding behind a still hydrangea branch, only her face, not her body depicted. Frightened of the very thing he wished to paint, Cezanne executed Hortensia Fiquet, (*moi*) with classical linear brushwork.

That night, I drifted off into what promised to be a restful sleep. I have been sharing a bed with my artist lover for over a year now. Him, an aspiring painter, me, an aspiring artist's model. Living secretly in sin... C'est la vie! It is Paris! It is 1870! Vin rouge coloured my cheeks and sent me to sleep, but a few hours later, I was awake again, with a dry mouth. The moonlight bouncing off the polished wood bed illuminated Cézanne's small, pinched face. His gentle breeze of breath blew his whiskers, yes, Cézanne, I hope one day you will make me Madame, I am prepared to wait the time it takes you to create twenty-seven oil paintings... In the early hours, I drifted off. The baking bread fragrance from the nearby boulangerie filled me, soothed me, but a few moments later, I was dreaming again! 'Non! Nonmademoiselle! Non! You are making a spectacle of yourself!'
'Wake up Hortense! Wake up, my flower!'
I opened my eyes, the sun was bright, I had slept, what time was it? The dream had recurred again, so vivid, so *unrealistic!*
'What were you dreaming about? You were shouting!' Cézanne asked, his face illustrated a mix of concern and fatigue.
'What was I shouting?'

'Errr, I, I was sleeping myself, some numbers... Two thousand and something? Does that mean anything to you?'

'Non' I shied into my nightshirt. I am an elegant, artist's model, not a bookbinding fishwife with night terrors.

I left my artist lover smoking and painting that morning. He said not to worry, and that he had a surprise for me.

I walked to work the same way, past the decorated doors, rose petals scattering the road like dramatic brushstrokes. What could the surprise be? I clock-watched the day away, self-absorbed in the fantasy of surprise jewellery. An engagement ring? I know he has his stuffy father's money to spend... But those women! The women in my dream, what does this mean? Posing contorted women objectifying themselves with untenable images of beauty. What does this mean?

'Bonsoir my flower! I have been waiting for you!' Cézanne met me at the door, he was dressed in a suit, not a paint mark on him, his kiss brushed my face, with the fragrance of turpentine. We made our way into the centre of Paris. Quelle surprise! We were going to the Annual Salon. Cezanne has been submitting here since 1863, submitting, while art snobs do their rejecting. Formulating his own style, gradually dissenting further away from tradition. I belong here, though. An artist's model. Most of the paintings, once exhibited, become commissions. The predictable style of the nude genre, always female, staring back at us, their pretty, unrealistic faces, their neat hair, their smooth brushwork, their dreamy expressions, hiding the very essence of what they are... A painting! Cézanne has been here longer than me, he should know, surely he knows. I look again, at these objectified women. Where do they get these models from? Frolicking about in the countryside, in the nude? Then it hit me...

'Hortense, wake up!'

I was being revived, by Cézanne, trying not to make a scene. I got up from the cold white floor, and we scurried away, this was our style, secret rendezvous. In a quiet cafe, I explained my dreams.

'I looked at those women, those statuesque poses, I was taken right back to my vivid recurring nightmares' I whispered, Cézanne nodded, his face illustrated the usual mix of concern and shame.

'It is always in the future, two thousand and something, it is always women, holding up shiny rectangular objects in their hands, posing, alone, in front of their own mirrors... and some of them have paid! Paid vast amounts of money with strange looking notes. Their hair and makeup altered with light and dark brushstrokes, a bit like those painted nudes, you see! And what is Facebook? What is Instagram?'

Cézanne nodded slowly, pondering my distress.

'Why do you find this so upsetting? If these women are in the future, then surely they cannot hurt you, or me?'

My hidden face illustrated the usual mix of fear and obsession.

'Because, my love, these dreams are always one horrible *competition* for these women! They are under so much pressure to maintain the untenable image of beauty! It is taking over their lives! And they are doing this to *themselves!*'

I could not describe the made up women, with painted, idealised faces and pouted lips. I am French, but even I know it does not hurt to smile, once in a while. Then Cézanne said something which really was a surprise.

'My love! My Hortense, you truly have inspired me, where would I be without you?' Then I knew that my premonition of twenty-seven paintings, a baby and a house in the south was about to come true. Over the next few years, Cézanne, although frightened of women, painted his *impression* of women, with his painterly technique, naked, classless women with loose cascading carefree curls and dramatic brushstrokes. Women with ponderous physiques, bathing in the dark countryside. Strangely more realistic than the Paris Salon's idealised, objectified women, and more realistic than my premonition of fake women of the future taking 'selfies'.

Safari Type Trip

The Sunny down day centre provides therapeutic activity and social inclusion. What could be better than a day trip in the summer months to brighten everyone's mood?

The manager of the day centre, Sally, had called a meeting with the service user steering group to discuss the destination and delivery of this year's big summer day out.

'We could go somewhere local to keep costs down, there are plenty of activities. Look I've brought a leaflet in about an art exhibition of sculptures in the country park, there's a nice pub nearby that does food'

'A pub! Don't be so insensitive! You know I can't drink on these tablets!' Mavis said, the main spokesperson for the steering group.

'Well, we could go in just for food' Sally reasoned.

'Food! I thought we were taking free sandwiches provided by the canteen? We always have free sandwiches' Mavis folded her arms higher around her chest.

'And we don't want to be local, remember what happened at the Christmas Markets? My Clive just wandered off home, he thought we had come out to do the shopping' Rita represented the carers in the community.

'Oh dear, I'm sorry, I'm only trying to help, Brighten everyone's mood? What do you think, Preeti? Is there anywhere you would like to go?' Sally asked, already losing control of the summer trip meeting.

'What I would really like, is to go on a safari type trip' Preeti beamed a huge infectious smile, which no one could resist. Even Mavis started smiling.

'Well, that's agreed then! A safari type trip! Write that down Sally' Mavis bossed.

'I'm sure I have seen vouchers for a safari park' Rita said, they're everywhere, on cereal boxes, teabag boxes, and dishwasher tablet packets 'We could collect them and get half price entry'

'Don't be so insensitive, Rita, you know I don't have a dishwasher!' Mavis re-folded her arms.

Over the next few weeks, Rita started a collection of safari park vouchers. Clive was sick to the back teeth of eating cereal and drinking tea. Mavis was sick of doing the washing up.

Sally had hired a mini bus, but with Alicia on maternity leave, she was short handed to marshal the big summer day out.

'Why don't you just ask Keely?' Mavis interfered.

'Well, erm Keely doesn't have the proper training' dismissed Sally.

'Training?'

'Yes, first aid for example'

'First aid? That's discrimination, Sally. You can't prevent Keely from coming on the day trip just because she doesn't know how to give mouth to mouth'

'Pardon!'

'Social inclusion, you said this trip was about. So if any of us lot have a funny turn, we should just do what the rest of society do... dial 999' Mavis folded her arms up high, she knew which card to play with Sally.

'Are you scared of her? I'll go and ask her if you're worried'

'No! Mavis! There's really no need!' Sally called after Mavis, who was making her way towards Keely, leaving Sally redundant at the office door.

'Hello Rita, hello Clive' Sally was glad to see them.

'Hello, I've just been to Dennis to order the packed lunches for our big summer trip. He said you would have to sign the funding slip because he is not talking to Keely'

Word gets around pretty quickly at the Sunny Down day centre.

The weather report had been checked. The vouchers had been counted. The Big Summer day trip had arrived!

'Keely!'

'Hiya Sally, Mavis, budge up will you?'

'What are you wearing?'

'Well it's a day out isn't it? Mavis told me to blend in, what are *you* wearing, Sally?' Keely defended. She had a point, Sally would not 'blend in' to society. She looked like an undercover police officer.

'Right everyone, we're here!' Sally pulled the handbrake on, and switched the radio off, she turned around. Clive had fallen asleep. Rita had managed to knit twelve squares for her quilting club. Doris, Preeti, and her mother were chatting. Mavis was playing online bingo on her smartphone.

'I am gasping, can we get out now?' Keely said to Sally.

'Actually, I need you to come with me to pay for the tickets, I need a witness when any money is dealt with' Sally said, officially.

'No problem, I need to stretch my legs!'

At the ticket booth, Sally pulled the discount vouchers from her nondescript handbag. Keely produced lip gloss from her designer tote.

'Eight tickets please, may I use these half price vouchers?' Sally said, pushing them forwards.

'Adult tickets?'

'Yeeaaas'

'Sorry dear, these vouchers are 'kids go free' so one adult pays, one child goes free, see what I mean? So I can let you have one free ticket for yourself when your mother pays, deary, the rest will have to pay full price' The ticket lady waved her hand towards Keely.

'Mother! She's isn't my...'

'Say nothing!' Keely whispered in Sally's ear.

The pair made their way back to the minibus.

'Can we get out yet?' Doris asked, again. She had been asking to get out of the bus since they had left Sunny Down.

'Just as soon as I explain about the tickets, Doris'

'Yeah, we couldn't get half price, apart from Sally, she got a free ticket because the woman in the ticket booth thought she was a little girl... and... wait for it! She thought I was her mother!' Keely and the rest of the minibus burst out laughing.

The first part of the safari park was on foot, the aviary, housing parrots, birds of prey, even vultures. Most in cages, each boasted a placard of explanation.

'This is my favourite part' Preeti said.

In the owl enclosure, Clive and Rita were joined by Preeti and her mother. It had tawny owls, barn owls, and a Eurasian owl, but the cave type structure appeared empty.

'Just keep going, Sally, I'm getting a bit claustrophobic in here' Mavis shouted from the back. Then the cave suddenly went dark, robbed of its light because the owner of the cave had spread its magnificent wings wide, then silently shut them.

'OWWWLLLL!!' Preeti's mother screamed, clutching on to her daughter by her elbow. This was worse than claustrophobia, at least Mavis and Doris could hide behind Sally.

The confronting owl appeared to put its wings on its hips. Its eyes were as big as dinner plates. But Preeti matched its gaze, they were now at a stand-off. Preeti's mother screamed in fear behind her.

'By heck!' said Clive... He doesn't say much.

'It's how they sneak up on their prey, their wings don't make much sound' Preeti said.

This went on for what appeared to be ten minutes until Preeti's mother grabbed Rita's knitting by the needles, she threw them at the owl, and then the four of them scurried out of the enclosure, leaving the other four behind.

'I think she's angered it!'

'Don't be silly, Keely, look! Preeti's mother wouldn't make it on the cricket field, she stood on Rita's ball of wool when she tried to throw!' Sally picked up the knitting and turned to leave, but she too was met face to face by the owl.

'I don't think you're supposed to smoke in her' Keely said, just as Mavis flicked a flame out of her lighter. The owl spread its wings once again and flew to the top of the aviary. Now it was Sally's turn to scream as she ran away.

'Thanks, love' Rita said when she took her knitting off Sally, who struggled to compose herself.

'Can we drive around now?' Doris asked, always keen to race on to the next bit of the day.

'Hang on! What about our packed lunch? I'm starving!' Mavis said.

'It's only ten thirty in the morning!' Laughed Keely.

Seatbelts on, driving around Bison, Giraffes, different exotic looking cattle.

'What's that? Addax? It's an Addax, Clive' Rita provided a running commentary for her husband.

'Zebras! I love Zebras!' Preeti said.

'Are they supposed to get that close to the vehicles?' Sally panicked 'Doris! Shut your window!'

'Aww look at its nose, look at its head! It's like a horse!'

'Sally, she's got that zebra's head on her lap!' Keely whispered. Sally slammed the brakes and the startled zebra bared its teeth at Doris.

'Oh, it's breath! Get it away from me! Oh, it stinks!'

'Doris, I did tell you to shut your window!'

'Err excuse me! Don't shout at Doris' Mavis adopted her usual arm folded pose.

'Hang on' Keely took control of the situation, she opened up the packed lunch box 'Watercress? A box of watercress? That Dennis has finally lost it!' Keely threw the watercress past the zebra, who quickly lost interest in Doris, who in turn had lost interest in the zebra 'Oh Keely, pass me something to eat out of that box will you?'

'No! No, look we need to find a nice picnic table' Sally was exasperated.

'Monkeys!' Preeta gasped.

'Ahhhh! It's on your windscreen Ahhhh!' Mavis was not reacting well to the monkeys, Keely was laughing her head off.

'Keely! Stop laughing! We do not laugh at one another at the Sunny Down day centre!' Sally snapped. When she turned back, though, she was met face to face with three monkeys that had landed on the front windscreen of the mini bus, or as they saw it, a urinal. Sally started to cry, but everyone else was laughing, even Mavis. Then Doris undid her seatbelt and ran towards the front of the bus.

'Get it off me! Take it away from me! It's off! Sally, It's off!' She had taken a quiche from out of the packed lunch box and was waving it around. The sour smell that followed confirmed that the quiche was indeed off.

'Sally I think you need to do something' Rita said.

'Well, I am doing *something*! I'm trying to drive around this monkey enclosure! I can't see where I'm going!' Struggling not to swear, Sally had completely lost it.

Keely tried to help Sally, but it was too late. Doris opened the window again and beckoned one of the monkeys as if it was a domesticated pet.

'Come on love, do you want some quiche?' Doris cooed.

'NO! Doris, don't feed the animals!' Sally slammed the brakes on, Rita dropped a stitch in her knitting, and Doris dropped the sour smelling quiche into the monkey enclosure.

'Doris!' Sally was at the end of her tether.

'I'm going to have to retrieve that quiche from outside, we're not allowed to feed the monkeys!' Sally said.

'I know but, you're not supposed to leave your vehicle either!' Keely was making sense.

But Sally was gone, slamming the sliding door behind her. They all watched as at least fifty monkeys jumped all over Sally, and all over the quiche.

'This is partly my fault you know' Keely whispered to Mavis 'I told Dennis I wouldn't go out with him last week, I think he has tampered with our packed lunches'

Mavis burst out laughing again.

When Sally returned to the van (after fighting her way back) she was covered from head to toe in monkey poo, mud, and the remainder of the quiche. At least Doris had shut her window.

Keely offered to drive the mini bus back home. Mavis spent the journey consoling the nervous wreck - that was Sally.

Later that same day, on return to the Sunny Down day centre. The day trippers were met at the door by Mike the manager, Sally's boss.

'Sally, you're late back, you know the protocol, telephone ahead. Anyway, there is something I need to speak to you all about. I realise it's been a long day' He raised an eyebrow at Sally.

When everyone had sat down in their own designated and familiar chairs, Mike the manager cleared his throat and announced:

'I'm afraid it's bad news... I've been to a meeting this morning, and there have been further cuts. From today, there can be no more day trips, I'm very sorry'

There was not even a pause, Mike the manager was met by a loud chorus of:

'Hurrah!'

Italian Elvis

Anthony had always loved singing. His Dad's side of the family was Italian, his Mother's Welsh. Anthony was very special. Welsh-Italian heritage meant that he was genetically double loaded to be a talented tenor.

When he was a boy, during the lengthy school summer holidays, his Nonna Francesca would come to stay. She would entertain Anthony all day, teaching him the skills and secrets involved in the art of cooking Italian food. Every day she put on an Operatic performance in the kitchen. A virtuoso herself, Nonna Francesca knew that all cooking rituals required rhythm. Anthony's spaghetti making classes were delivered by Nonna Francesca accompanied by Elvis songs, sung like a soprano. She would tease him, of course with a pretend language barrier. Even though Nonna Francesca knew all the words to every Elvis song, she had managed to convince young Anthony that she spoke very little English, the result being that Anthony was very well behaved. He was rewarded with a teaspoon of tiramisu, a forbidden grown up dessert, which was soon to become his favourite.

Time moved on, gradually Nonna Francesca and her Elvis gnocchi lessons were no longer required in the summer holidays, but Nonna and her grandson's bond remained strong. She was his biggest fan and during Anthony's latter teenage years, Nonna Francesca would be in the crowd of every single reality TV singing competition that Anthony entered. He went in for them all. Some had chairs, some had crowds. Unfortunately, he failed to get through to the second stage of any of the fame generating, rating hungry shows. The only time he appeared on television was when he was standing behind someone being interviewed. Nonna Francesca still thought he was the most wonderful singer ever, even better than the King himself. Cheering 'bravo' (and shaking her fist whilst cursing in Italian at the judges) After a few years, Anthony came to realise that Nonna Francesca's unconditional support and persuasion, had set him up to fail. The only songs he knew how to sing were Elvis songs. Apparently, there was no current gap in the modern music market for impersonators. Queuing up, and getting turned away did not pay the bills either. Actually, he was still living at home, but he wanted to learn how to drive. Anthony dug into his reserves and with the skills he had learned as a child, he managed to land a job as a chef. In a world of NVQ's and apprenticeships, Anthony had to push his Italian heritage to one side and work at the local conveyor belt carvery. This pleased his entire family, supporting him again by booking the extra large round table every Sunday. If only they could hear his new work colleagues calling him 'Tony' rather than his given name of 'Anthony' they would realise that he was unhappy in his work, singing in the kitchen 'Are You Lonesome, Tonight?' to the turkey.

'You should go in for one of those talent shows, Tony' Said Mandy, one of the waitresses.

Oh dear, Anthony was ambivalent initially about another admirer, a female fan, infatuated only with his singing. But over time, Anthony (or 'Tony') got to like Mandy, he would look forward to going to work, just so that he could see her. He even plucked up the courage to sing 'the wonder of you' but when she arrived at the kitchen, Mandy just laughed. Nevertheless, she really was his tiramisu, his object of affection. Anthony thought about her a lot, how he could work his way around to asking her out. But every time he had the chance, he bottled it. His Italian genes had let him down.

Sunday roasts came and went. Anthony continued to sing in the kitchen, the peas and carrots refused to join in. He was not part of the workplace gossip, he was busy counting cranberries for the sauce. One day, the head barman, Nigel popped his head into the kitchen.

'I've come to invite you to my stag do, we're going to Tenerife, are you up for it, Tony?' Anthony raised his eyebrows, pouted his lips and nodded:

'I s'pose' Anthony answered, not thinking to ask who the bride was.

'Oh, and as Mandy likes your singing so much, how are you fixed for doing a bit of wedding singing at the do?'

Nigel was marrying Mandy! Oh dear, Anthony was heartbroken, but he had never been asked to sing at a wedding before. He adopted bravado, puffed out his chest and said:

'I'm sorry, I've kind of turned my back on performing'

'Oh go on Tony, help a mate out? Do you know any other songs other than Elvis Presley though?'

'I s'pose so, although no, I only know how to sing Elvis' Anthony replied to his love rival in the style of a true divo.

'Hey you're not crying are you?' Nigel handed Anthony a piece of kitchen roll.

'No, it's the onion gravy, gets me every time' Mandy had her hen do first. Learner plates, embarrassing photographs, and hangovers were strewn all over the staff quarters of the carvery on her return.

Then it was Nigel's stag do. Ten men packed onto a budget airline headed for the sun and sangria. At Nigel's insistence, they all had a special stag do t-shirt made with their nickname printed on the back. Usually, their own surname with a 'y' added. (Browny, Henny and so on) Nigel had 'Nige' and Anthony's nickname for the weekend was 'Elvis'. In true 'Brits abroad' style, Nigel's stag do went down with a 'what happens in Tenerife, stays in Tenerife' mantra. Although, there were no anecdotal tales to keep secret. Try as they might, Nigel and his mates were not as talented or amusing as they thought they were. On the last night of debauchery, the lads were instructed to put their T-shirts back on for the final hoorah. Despite their boasted collective stamina, and wolf cries to 'bring it' they were all drunk, deflated and ready for bed by about 10.30pm.

Anthony was hungry, he spotted a pizza takeaway. It is a well-known fact that everyone loves Italian food, and without Italian food, there would be no pizza takeaways. Whilst he was waiting for his 12" Hawaiian (not *traditionally* an Italian flavour) a woman approached him from the neighbouring bar.

'Excuse me... Why are you wearing an Elvis T-shirt?'

Now Anthony had consumed at least two Jaeger-bombs and several gallons of beer, but thanks to his genes, was able to manipulate his vocal chords around a beautifully spoken answer.

'Oh, what a coincidence!' the woman said, in beautifully pronounced Spanglish 'We are advertising for an Elvis singer for our bar' Despite the excessive alcohol intake, and before Anthony knew it, he had completed an audition and had been given the job on the spot. He had sung one of Nonna Francesca's favourites, 'Suspicious Minds', a quick but impressive rendition, he didn't want his 12" Hawaiian pizza to go cold. Anthony was hired on the spot. A phone call home, an emotional farewell with Nigel, Anthony was ready to start his new life.

In the beginning, he was really enjoying his new job, pretending to be someone else, there was no training required as Anthony knew all the words to each and every one of Elvis Presley's songs. The bar was part of the Hotel Cleopatra, maybe he should have known better because everyone knows that Cleopatra was responsible for Antony's downfall. The first outfit he was provided with was black leather trousers and matching jacket, he looked amazing, much like Elvis' '1968 Comeback Special' look. Unfortunately, the outfit proved to be too hot, a bit like the barmaid who had been sent over to persuade him to audition. In the end, he had to settle for the 'young Elvis' look. Jeans, white socks, black shoes and a T-shirt.

Soon, Anthony's job became his 'job' he missed home. At one time all he had dreamed of was singing, but as he looked at the holidaymakers in the audience, middle-aged women with their blouses tucked into their knickers he wondered what Nonna Francesca would think if she could see him. He asked if he could wear the '1970s Elvis look' the draughtiness of the trousers might be a bit cooler. But this was not allowed, another Elvis already rocked that look, on the other side of the strip. At the Volcano bar, pulling in the crowds was yet another Elvis impersonator. Dirty Elvis. Where Anthony was billed as 'Young Elvis', his rival was billed as a 'comedian'. He was ancient and so were his jokes, he was a good turn, even though most of the audience were thinking 'you can't tell jokes like that anymore, not in this century!'. Dirty Elvis got to wear the 1970s look, wig included. His vocal range was limited, relying heavily on an over exaggerated American accent. The drinks at the Volcano bar were expensive, but not watered down, making his performance all the more enjoyable.

Anthony Brylcreemed his hair as usual, and started his routine with the usual '(Marie's the name) His Latest Flame'. Now that Anthony knew that Dirty Elvis was singing, a bit further down the strip, he could hear him in his own song's segue. But when the lights lit up the audience for the sing-a-long 'The Wonder of You' Anthony noticed something wonderful himself; it was Nonna Francesca! Although Nonna usually enjoyed holidaying in Italy, she had decided this year to visit her Anthony in Tenerife. She had stories about Mandy and Nigel's wedding, it turned out alright in the end, they hired a DJ instead. And some other news, Anthony's Grampa Owen - his mother's father had returned to Wales from New Zealand. He had been sheep farming for the past twenty years but had decided to retire.

Nonna Francesca had smuggled Italian biscotti and coffee in her case. The two of them explored the island, they even hired a scooter made for two. Nonna Francesca was not impressed with the pizza takeaway, but they enjoyed some lovely seafood and Canarian potatoes. Every night, she cheered Anthony's singing 'Bravo!' (whilst giving the evil eye to anyone who was not clapping)

On Anthony's night off, they went for a walk down the strip towards the beach. It was a beautiful night. The road and pavement shone gleaming white, the holidaymakers enjoyed ice-cream and caricatures. And then it happened. Dirty Elvis had just come to the end of one of his songs in the open plan bar when he looked out onto the street and he saw a beautiful Italian lady; it was Nonna Francesca. To Anthony's horror, his grandmother returned the admiring glance. There ensued a second glance and a smile. Dirty Elvis winked and smooched 'Uhh huh huh' into his microphone. The whirlwind of attraction was as dramatic as Puccini's Tosca. That was the start of it...

Broken hearted once again, cursed with passionate and dramatic genes, Anthony left Tenerife. Nonna Francesca would forgive him eventually for their crossed words at the airport:

'He's completely bald under that Elvis wig you know!' Anthony had protested. He knew, though, that his parents would welcome him home with open arms.

Not just his parents, Gramps Owen had returned home and just as Anthony had remembered him, had taken up residence in the family shed.

'So, he got to wear the cool 70s outfit, see' Anthony finished filling in his gramps about Tenerife as he drank his camping stove cup of tea 'I don't know what I'm going to do now!' 'I'll teach you the family business, sheep farming, let you know all their little secrets' Gramps Owen said.

'Sheep don't have secrets, Gramps!' Anthony said with mature concern for his grandfather's mind.

'Oh yes, they do, Anthony!'

'I thought it was between the sheep and the sheepdog?'

'You're right, it is, but a farmer only wants happy sheep and I know what makes them happy. They love to be serenaded, you know, they love a bit of singing'

Oh no... Anthony thought, not this again. He really had decided to turn his back on singing, especially Elvis songs. Now here was his Grandpa about to employ him as a singing shepherd. Visions of Dirty Elvis stood before him like a hunk of burning disappointment- was this how his life was going to turn out?

'Are you alright son? You've gone all quiet?'

'Yes sorry Gramps, what were you about to tell me about sheep and singing?' Anthony let out an involuntary sigh as he spoke, he was as drained as the bars in Tenerife after Nige's stag do. Gramps peeped out of the shed door to check that no one was listening, and out of the corner of his mouth, he whispered to Anthony 'Secret is, they like a few Tom Jones songs!'...

Cringe-Worthy People

'It's fine, my Mum is cool you'll love her. Although, I don't think my grandparents are ready for you just yet!'

It was the first time that Chloe had brought her boyfriend, Joe home, they had met at university.

'Hello?' Chloe shouted to check if anyone was at home 'I'm sure I saw my Dad's car outside, you'll like him, just talk to him about heavy metal ... anyway, do you want a cup of tea?'

'Err, just water please'

Chloe ran the tap, but before she managed to reach a glass, she was distracted by her Smartphone buzzing.

'That's been ringing since we got off the train, Chloe!'

'Oh, it's Molly from over the road, hello! Oh! Sorry, I totally forgot! Err no, I've brought Joe home to meet my parents...' Chloe held her noisy mobile away from her ear. Joe raised his eyebrows at the noise.

'Hang on, Molly' Chloe had some negotiating to do 'Joe, would you mind waiting here for an hour or so? I promised Molly that I would go with her to Brownies, we used to volunteer together before I started Uni...' Chloe pleaded to Joe. Poor Joe. He was torn between impressing Chloe, who he was a little bit in love with, and the embarrassment of being left alone in her house, waiting for her parents to arrive home.

'Yeah ok,' Joe decided.

There was an angry knocking at the door, it was Molly, Chloe ignored her shouts of *'You promised to come to Brownies with me! I've had to do it on my own whilst you've been at university!'*

'You can go and wait in my bedroom if you want, Joe, second door on the right upstairs' Chloe put her coat back on. Joe made his way upstairs, he could hear running water and in-shower singing of .. what was that? Guns N' Roses? Second door on the right? All the doors were shut. There were only four doors upstairs. She did say second door on the right, didn't she? Joe said to himself... Oh... too late! The bathroom door opened, steam billowed out onto the landing, a man was walking straight towards him wearing nothing but a towel on his head, towel drying his lengthy locks into a birds nest.

'Hello?' Joe panicked.

The giant jumped and screamed like a girl, hurriedly wrapping the towel around his middle. 'Who are you?'

'I'm Joe, Chloe has had to go out... she told me to wait in her bedroom, was that AC/DC you were singing?'

The giant frowned, but then eased his face into a rescue of recognition.

' Ahh Joe, I'm Richard, Chloe's dad' he held out his hand to shake Joe's hand but quickly withdrew it because of the slipping towel 'Well, her bedroom is that one, get yourself a beer from the fridge, Joe, and by the way, I never sing Def Leppard in the shower'

Joe turned and opened Chloe's bedroom door, it was a bit stiff, he struggled to get in, pushing the door open against an immense pile of clothes, just as the front door opened again.

'Bonjour ... I mean Bon .... soir!' a voice sang from downstairs 'Who's is this bag? I nearly tripped over it! Is Chloe home?' It was Chloe's mum back from her 'beginner's French' lesson at the local library. Now that Chloe had started University, she was free to learn French on a Thursday. No one answered her salutations, though.

Joe thought about going downstairs. Should he introduce himself to Chloe's mum? Get in her good books? Or should he just wait for Chloe to return? Joe slid down the partition wall of the 1970's semi detached house, he did not mean to have his ear to it, but it was the only space left in this very untidy bedroom. Then he overheard something terrible...
'Bonjour Monsieur!"
Chloe's mum was now in the other bedroom with Chloe's naked dad...
'Gerroff! ... I don't think I like French Joanne!" The heavy metal voice shouted.
Ah! Joanne, that's her name. Joe thought to himself, still hiding in Chloe's bedroom.
'What did you learn in French lesson today then?'
'We were practising the accent, you should hear this bloke, he sounds proper French, you can almost see his baguettes'
'What?'
Joe did not know why he was still listening and tried to wish himself out of the situation. His potential escape route - Chloe's bedroom window was hidden behind an assault course of manicure kits, clothes, lava lamps and hair straighteners. He decided to man up and go downstairs for that glass of water he had been promised earlier.

But back inside the parent's bedroom down the hall, that squeaky step on the staircase could be heard over all the giggling and French accents.

'Shhh! Did you hear that? Shhh, Richard, we're being burgled! Quick! Put some clothes on!' Joanne said, panicking.

It dawned on Richard where the sound was coming from, and he explained to Joanne about their visitor... but it was too late for Joe. Chloe was back at the front door, and she had two more people with her... She glared at Joe with emergency eyes, mouthing the words: *'GO BACK UPSTAIRS AND HIDE IN MY BEDROOM... PLEEEEEAAAASE!'*

Chloe turned to the two people who were climbing over the front doorstep. Joe returned to the bedroom and continued to be bombarded by different voices.

"COME IN GRANDMA AND GRANDAD. I'M NOT SURE IF MY MUM IS HOME YET, BUT YOU SIT IN THE FRONT ROOM AND I'LL MAKE YOU A CUP OF TEA!" Chloe over exaggerated, for Joe's benefit.

"We're old, Chloe but I'm not completely deaf," Grandma said.

"Shit! Richard!... It's my parents! Why are you still naked?!"

"Who's is this coat, Chloe?" Grandma picked Joe's coat up off the dining room chair.
"Oh it's mine, look" Chloe put it on.
"Is that how they're wearing them these days? Three sizes too big?' Grandma quizzed.
As Chloe's parents made their way downstairs, producing, even more embarrassing conversations. All Joe could do was wedge himself in next to a bean-bag, wait for Chloe to rescue him, and look forward to the day when Chloe meets *his* family, now they *really are* cringe worthy.

The Causeway

'Stop!'
'Stop! Please stop, you can't even sing!' She
was getting on his last nerve. The repetitive
radio had dropped out of signal forty miles
previously and she had started singing almost
immediately. Now, she was three beats away
from 'Kumbaya' - enough to test the patience
of any saint.
'Excuse me!' She huffed 'I'm just trying to
make the journey go quicker' Folded arms and
frowning, every married couple deserves an
argument on Christmas day. Smug
congratulations steamed up the car window
because they had remained friendly until the
afternoon.
Rain whipped their car like aluminium foil on
a baking sheet. The road ahead threatened an
abyss of darkness. A wash of burnt umber and
aquamarine where tarmac hit the sky. Miles
and miles of Roman straight, the ancient path
that does not suffer foolish corners. Soon,
although it had felt like years, their car met
with others, greeted by acid xenon light
emitting taillights.
'Traffic? On Christmas day? Where are all
these people driving to?'

'Same place as us!'
'What? Your parent's house?'
The very northeast boasts freedom from light pollution and no digital signal either. No service stations... well not on Christmas day, anyway.
'You'd better turn the engine off! We don't want to run out of petrol!' her survival instincts kicked in, already armed with a packet of ten 2-ply tissues, for roadside toilet emergencies.
'It'll be OK, we'll be moving along soon' his reassurance unmatched by his fingers, manipulating the unconscious electronic map on the dash.
'Is your phone dead too?'
'Yes,' her response as flat as their batteries.
The roadside had never been inspected so closely, by a creeping car. He slowly slid his window inside the door, his head soon became wet from craning, like a dog outside to see as far as he could.
'You're not gonna believe this' he laughed 'there's a workman up there holding up a stop sign!'
'What! Road works? On Christmas day? I hope he's getting paid double!'
'Double and time in lieu!'
'What can be so urgent on Christmas day?' She huffed, with middle-aged intolerance.

'Potholes' he asserted, with absolute conviction.

Idyllic in the summer months, when sunset kisses dawn, the same journey in winter provides a daunting drive when afternoon hours could be midnight outside. Two hours along the pinnacle 'A' road feel like two days, the corner of the country, the Holy Island, where tides create a daily new nation.

Aluminium foil whipped a baking sheet, awaiting their arrival, their second Christmas day in twenty-four hours. Eat, drink, sleep, repeat (provided they arrive there).

It was her turn to venture out into the rain, to see for herself the cause of their disdain.

'Oh, my... flip! You're right! He's holding up a stop sign!' She gasped, with rhetoric, as though he had lied and wedged herself back into the passenger seat.

'I read this article about those men who do the road works'

'Highway engineers?'

'Yes, highway thingies, well anyway, it was saying, there was an epidemic a while ago, they were using speed, you know, amphetamine, only so they could stay awake all night, they work nights, see'

'Yes, not as much traffic at night, they can get more potholes fixed'

'Right well, obviously drugs are illegal, no what d'you call it? Manufacturing standards, so they got a dodgy batch, right. It wasn't speed they were taking, it was LSD! They carried on working, apparently didn't stop, until there were stop signs everywhere'
'Are you sure? I don't believe that!'
'I read it!'
'Well, it must be true then!'
Meanwhile, at their destination, the food was going cold and wine was getting flat.
Presents clock watched from underneath wrapping and cello tape.
'Is this the only way? I'm sure your dad was going on about a coastal road route'
'Oh, God! What like that short cut home from Chillingham Castle? It wasn't even a road!'
'Remember! That bloke stopped us in his Vauxhall Astra, I thought he was going to murder us!'
'Oh! Don't be soft, he was asking for directions. You always think that! You always think people are either murderers... or on drugs!
'I do not! He was a local! Why would he need directions?' She folded her arms even tighter.
'How did you know he was local? I hope you didn't start talking to him? He would've been there all day!' He really should learn to talk under his breath, for his own sake.

'It was the accent if you don't mind! He called me 'Pet' ... they call everyone 'Pet' up here'
She really should learn how to turn down the volume.
He answered her with a sharp u-turn in the road. The queuing drivers free to treat the road as they pleased, the suspicious stop sign produced no oncoming traffic.
'He knows what he's doing, he's a good driver, he knows what he's doing' She repeated to herself, accompanied by breathing she had learned at Thursday yoga. When she opened her eyes, she was met by the greys and blacks of winding country roads, a tunnel of tree branches, taking her memory to the safety of childhood illustrations.
'He knows where he's going'
But he didn't. Miles and miles, the day escaping them, the tide rising somewhere in the distance, like a competition that cannot be won. Turns of junctions - now in darkness. The mobile phone signal still dubious, reluctant to accept defeat, he lied to his wife.
'Don't worry, when we turn the next corner, we'll be back in civilisation, I expect we'll see a sign for the causeway'

The next corner arrived, with its promised sign. Twenty-year-old graffiti raised a smile, '*STOP! HAMMER-TIME*' But their smiles swiftly faded as they realised they had come full circle and met the same traffic, and the same highway engineer holding up the same stop sign.

The parents, presents, and food still waiting on the other side of the causeway in anxious anticipation, countryside retirement threatened Christmas day alone. Every married couple deserves an argument on Christmas day.

A Fresh Start

A repeat blood test? I hope I pass this time! She makes it sound like a competition that nurse...

Graham was sure it was 'just to check' and assumed there had been a mix-up at the hospital. The nonsense the nurse said to him had gone in one ear and out the other. He looked away and presented his arm. The tourniquet snapped when she had finished. The nurse peered at Graham over the top of her spectacles.

'Pop on the scales for me'

Graham stood on the rubber step and watched the needle wobble, then fix on one number. Next came the Velcro blood pressure cuff. The tapping of keys and Graham's statistics were fixed in the computerised medical notes. Advice to diet and exercise three times a week were dismissed during the drive home. He wanted a full English, coffee with two sugars and ... Graham's car smashed into his garage door... He had been distracted by this morning's upset and was not paying attention. Whilst assessing the damage, he noticed leaflets protruding from his letterbox. Chinese takeaway, landscape gardening, and ...

'*THE FRESH START SPA AND GYM*' half price membership offer.

That night he did not sleep well, imagining his blood sample in transit with the hospital porters. He had never had an accident with his car like that before and blamed the nurse for putting him in a mood about his health. Refusing to be beaten, he decided to join the gym.

Graham spent the first week on the treadmill, listening to women gossiping. They had plenty to say about people who were strangers to Graham, and he was finding it tedious. But all was not lost because soon he found the spa! Graham could sit in the sauna all morning, spectacles steamed up, sweat rolling down his stomach. He became a regular. Everyone knew him. The gym instructor even invited him to join the men's over fifties cardio club. Graham said he would think about it.

After a few months, Graham could tell he was getting healthier because he could reach down to pick up a shiny object on the path leading up to the gym. It was someone's membership card... A woman's! Graham flipped it over in his hand, breathless from the exertion of bending down. The eyes in the picture smiled back up at him, captured in a frame of strawberry blonde hair. The name on the card read 'Yvonne' date of birth ... only five years younger than me! She's lovely! Graham popped the card into his tracksuit bottom pocket.

Inside, Yvonne was the first person he saw. Graham's heart started thumping. He should have returned her card to her, but she caught him staring, and seemed to frown, before disappearing into the women's changing rooms. Graham thought about handing the card in at reception, but they were busy stacking energy drinks...

Graham spent the following fortnight looking at Yvonne's photograph. A souvenir of his time at the Fresh Start gym. Her face smiling up at him, 'My Yvonne', he imagined. By the fourteenth day of abstinence from the gym, Graham had invented an entire fantastical life for himself and Yvonne, living harmoniously in their imaginary home. He even imagined they would get a puppy, a dog would definitely give them exercise.

The letterbox clattered and brought Graham back to the reality of his lonely house. It was another invitation from the GP surgery.

Yvonne had spent the same fortnight searching for her gym membership card. She had received the same 'half price offer' leaflet that Graham had, and decided to go for it. She would not usually take any notice of junk mail, but after enduring a terrible year, with a relationship breakdown she saw the leaflet as a 'sign'. Her friends had told her she should 'start doing things for herself'. After a few months, Yvonne started to enjoy exercising, it started to pay off, and this meant it was time to treat herself to a new swimming costume. Bright green, to match her eyes. But Yvonne was worried that this would bring her unwanted admiration. A lot of men went to the Fresh Start gym, and although she had not joined with the intention of meeting anyone, she needed time before she could date, or even return a smile to a man.

Meanwhile, Graham had now perfected the skill of keeping a close distance just behind Yvonne and had decided to return to his gym regime. Hiding behind the indoor palm tree in the Fresh Start gym's entrance, he was just far enough away to listen in:

"No one's handed my membership card in then? Oh dear, I'll have to pay the replacement fee then" Yvonne's voice was as musical as Graham had imagined. Sweat pumped out of his palms, and his mouth was dry. Now was his chance! But how could he say anything without admitting he had kept her membership card?

He started to feel funny, his head started spinning, he felt a bit sick. Then a loud thudding sound followed...

......

The paramedic wheeled Graham into the ambulance, explaining that as Graham had fallen without warning it was better to get 'checked out'.

"Are you his wife?" He asked Yvonne.

"Oh! ... No! He gave me a fright when he fell over, I just came over to help... I did a first aid course at work last week, the staff dialled 999!" Yvonne gushed, her face blushed.

"That's strange, is this your gym membership card? He was holding it a moment ago!"

"Oh, that is strange! I've been looking for that!" Yvonne looked at the paramedic. What a hero, she thought to herself... "I'm ... not married actually"

All Graham could do was lie there inside the ambulance and pretend to be unconscious, whilst the paramedic smiled at Yvonne, who smiled back at him with her beautiful face and strawberry blonde hair.
Graham was not the only one who was looking for a fresh start...

Finding the Right Name

'Stop!'
'Don't do that! Noooo! Stop it! Good girl!
Who's a good girl?'
My forelock is vigorously ruffled like a child
at a birthday party. I mouth her hand with my
teeth and tongue. I'm so eager to please but so
confused. Yesterday, I got a treat for going to
the toilet in exactly the same place. It's a bit of
chicken from the cold, white cupboard, or a
bone-shaped biscuit from the box on the
window shelf. I've been observing; it doesn't
matter what I do, or how many 'coos' I cause,
each treat depends on how close she is to
each...

'CAT!... CAT IN YOUR GARDEN! CAT, CAT, CAT!' I bark. I don't think she understands dog. Now, where was I? Oh yes, the quality of treat is not equivalent to the cuteness of my behaviour. I have an arsenal of tools at my disposal. Toilet (solid and liquid) biting and not biting. Fetching balls. Looking cute. Walking nice. Being a good girl. Oh and let's not forget; Causing guilt. Yes, bigger, sweeter bone shaped biscuits arrive in my cage, just before she abandons me, when she shuts the front door, with her on the other side of it. When she returns, I make sure she has not forgotten who I am, eager to please with jumping and licking and jumping, like a long lost reunion. One thing worries me, though, when she does return, she seems to have forgotten my name. I don't hear her shout 'Stop' for ages.

My Dam told us pups, she said 'You will be given a name by your human. So listen out for a word they repeat lots' I was listening intently of course, my head cocked to one side, then I remember the next bit 'Girls usually get a name with two sounds, like 'Millie' and boys usually get a name with one sound, such as 'Titch' my brother had lost interest by this point, his teeth, like needles sinking into her nips. 'Stop!' she yelped. And soon, we were out of that whelping box, shivering in fear all the way to our new upside down worlds. Listening carefully to find the right name. That's why I think my human might be stupid. I think she thinks I'm a boy. A boy called Stop.

We get along ok. She likes the sound I make when I'm drinking water, and I like the sound of the puppy food tin opening.

Today she has shut us both out on the other side of the door. She fastens the silver clasp on my collar, opens another door, throws a treat onto a seat. She is all jangly with keys and poo bags, appointment cards and phones. She keeps trying to take photos of me, but I just run under her feet, she just gets the end of my wagging tail, so much fun.

'Good girl! Come on! Get in the car!'

Does she expect me to climb up there? I'm so confused. Last time I was inside this moving machine, I was wrapped up in a towel that smelt like home. I put my head on one side, she looks at me like she's going to eat me, and I carry on messing about around her ankles. 'Stop! Stop biting me!' She sings. Then I am scooped up around my middle, her silly sticky lips kiss the top of my head and all of a sudden, I'm inside the moving machine. We rumble along. I watch her every move turning a big wheel. The door opens.
'SAVE YOURSELF! SAVE YOURSELF! SAVE YOURSELF!' I bark. Why bother getting a puppy when you don't even know how to speak dog? Some people!
'Stop! Stop barking! It's only a lorry driving past!' She says, well how does she expect me to react? This is the biggest road I have ever seen, I trot along beside her, and soon we're inside.

'Smelllllllls! Smelllllllls and more smellllllls' I sniff around the corner of every floor, while she is preoccupied, giving a name in at the desk. We are obviously not here for me because I don't hear her say 'Stop!' Just as I'm about to add my own smell to this heavily scented linoleum, she responds to a new voice, that has opened another door. How exciting! But wait, I smell fear inside. The fear of pets, who have walked through this door, never to return. I position my four little legs taught, stick my bum on the floor. Stupid human cannot tell I don't want to go into this room. Can't you see? I look like a triangle! My tail is down, my teeth are barred. Still, she drags my lead towards this scary stranger. 'STOP! STOP!' I bark.

'Just relax the lead, and let her come and say hello' The white coated human says. *Finally!* Someone who can speak dog! Someone who knows I'm a bitch! I have to sit on a table, have a sharp thing prodded into my neck, get stroked a lot. Nothing to it really, the treats here are gooooood! And I was right! We are here for her! She talks a bit, and then it's the white coat's turn to talk, then it's my human again. I turn my head from one side to the next, listening in to their game of talking tennis. Then the door opens, the white coat looks busy, that taking it in turns to talk has taken too long. I'm free! Nothing to it! Phew! Confusing pissy fear smells ... Hello! Who are you?

'STOP, STOP... STOP, STOP!' He barks. 'Hello? I only want to say hello!' I sprinkle excitedly across the floor with puppy dog eyes. Before I know it, I'm scooped up by his nose under my back legs, he sniffs my undercarriage, to check if I'm a girl, my stupid human has confused everyone, by calling me Stop.

'Stop that, *again!'* His human is wagging a finger in his face.

Again? That's not a name? And how do they know me? Stop?

'Pleased to meet you, Again, the white coat's free now, nothing to it!' I bark a little bark at him, before I'm dragged along the floor, and out of the door.

Spoofapaedia .
Article
<u>Wrapped in Plastic and the Stiffadoms (band)</u>
This article is a work of fiction, about the imaginary girl band Wrapped in Plastic. For the real band, or the Twin Peaks reference, please consult your internet browser.

Background information

Origin   Manchester, UK.

Genres   Metal, Girl band metal, modern day riot grrl.

Years active   Forever in their minds.

Labels   Who in their right mind? (Ltd.)

<u>History</u>

Wrapped in Plastic are a fictional all girl three piece rock band from Manchester, UK. Formed during the summer heavy metal festival weekend in the Midlands, during a day of sunshine and bravado. Lead singer Caroline McQueen had always been one glass of wine away from forming her own girl band. Heavily influenced by the riot girl scene of the early nineties, she met drummer Suzanne Strange, whilst passing the time in the portaloo queue singing Babes in Toyland songs. Joined by bass guitarist Leanne Hotter, (not just in the queue) the three-piece was formed, and named after the opening scene of David Lynch's Twin Peaks. Hotter later changed the name to the mouthful that was 'Wrapped in Plastic and the Stiffadoms'.

<u>Releases/ Discography</u>
"The Legend of Q-Man EP" (2016)
[That's it]

<u>Musical style.</u>

McQueen has often been quoted as comparing Wrapped in Plastic's noise to that of Courtney Love and Debbie Harry's love child, whereas, Strange states she actually *is* Courtney Love and Debbie Harry's love child. When asked, Hotter was trying on an electric blue spandex body stocking and was unable to comment. Nevertheless music journalists, haters and internet trolls have described them as 'all bite and no bark'. Strange, opting to play the drums so that she could sit down, saw herself as both good looking and talented, of which she is neither. In defence, McQueen, the brains behind the outfit whipped up considerable kudos for the band on social media and the likes of Everett True returned from journalistic retirement, just to write about them.

Hiatus

After a sell out UK tour in September of 2016, Wrapped in Plastic and the Stiffadoms' management were forced to quit the crazy scene of mid-life crisis girl band metal. The three piece themselves had mounting legal fees in the small claims court, due to disgruntled fans demanding refunds after short sets, and noise that even Goths could not resonate with. The original Q-Man tracked the band down, demanding royalties but unable to prove he was the *'Stranger with a vacant stare and really long hair'* he opted to settle out of court by agreeing to make guest appearances at any future shows. The actual band 'Wrapped in Plastic' also took issue with the three piece using their name. They decided to drop all charges of plagiarism, because any publicity is good publicity, right? However, after a string of unpaid bar bills, and a mountain of unsold merchandise, Wrapped in Plastic and the Stiffadoms are currently not speaking to each other on hiatus.

Reunion Tour

Rumours have been sweeping the mill in Manchester, prompted by McQueen, Strange and Hotter being spotted on three separate occasions buying three separate spandex leotards (the trademark look for the Q-Man tour). However, in the spring of 2017, reports that McQueen has accidentally formed a new band with her friend Carina Bass, they currently have plans for a two piece art installation show, based on screaming and pole dancing. Strange is currently resident in a rehabilitation facility receiving treatment for a secret drug addiction, so secret that even she didn't know about it. Hotter is currently pregnant with triplets, again, but in her mind, she is currently on their world tour.

Awards and Nominations
Zero.

Thank you for reading... Watch this space...

More by the author:
Piccalilli, a remembrance day short story.
Piccalilli is a short children's novel about Lillian, an eight year old girl who is missing her older brother, Joe. He has been serving in the army in World War One. When Lillian's parents receive a telegram informing them of the worst, Lillian discovers that Joe's spirit is living on in a series of comforting events.
Piccalilli was based around a true story, in memory of the author's family. Written originally for the author's mother, but published to remember those who lost their lives during World War One.
A short story that both children and adults can (hopefully) enjoy.

18039574R00142

Printed in Poland
by Amazon Fulfillment
Poland Sp. z o.o., Wrocław